one hit blunder

worst detective ever
book twelve

Christy Barritt

chapter
one

"LIFE FEELS like sand slipping through my fingers," I murmured as I pedaled down the dark road on my bike.

Tears streamed from my eyes and across my cheeks before blowing into my hair. They mixed with the fat raindrops that had just begun to fall from the autumn skies.

"I'm going to do this," I whispered. "I have no choice. I've lost everything, and now I'm a nobody."

I'd written everything out so people would understand my choices.

I was keenly aware of the pills jangling in my pocket.

Keenly aware of what I'd do with them.

As I passed over a small bridge crossing the marsh,

I suddenly jerked forward. My tire must have hit something.

The bike careened out of control.

I gripped the handlebars as I tried to keep it upright.

But it was too late.

The beach cruiser slammed into the cement curb at the side of the bridge.

I toppled over the handlebars, and my head banged the railing.

As I rolled over the edge, blackness tried to consume me.

Then I hit the frigid water. For an instant, I snapped back to life.

Everything felt vividly clear.

No! Not like this. This isn't how it's supposed to end!

I needed to pull myself up and out of the water. Even though it was only a foot deep, I was facedown.

But I couldn't move. My limbs wouldn't cooperate.

Water filled my lungs, and I couldn't breathe.

Darkness moved in. Squeezed around me. Then squeezed harder.

A gurgle sounded in my lungs.

Then my world went black.

I dropped the script on the kitchen countertop,

crossed my arms, and looked at my husband, Jackson. "This just doesn't ring true to me."

"How so?" Jackson needed to leave in a few minutes for a weeklong training session in Raleigh. Right now, he was finishing his morning coffee and staring at me like someone had released a loon in the house—and that loon was me.

"Something is . . . off. This scene just doesn't work." I plucked the script as if it had personally wronged me.

Jackson sauntered toward me and paused, tilting his head and leveling his gaze. "Joey, sweetheart, this isn't a script you can change. It's a biopic on a one-hit wonder. There's no changing the way Emma Jean Gibbons lived—or died."

I tried not to pout, but I was having trouble explaining my thoughts right now. Jackson liked to follow logic. I liked to follow my gut—and, to be honest, several popular TikTok creators. But that was mostly for fashion advice.

As a result, Jackson and I didn't always understand each other.

But I was trying really hard to let him into my head. He said my head was a scary place, and I had to agree. Thinking about crime around every corner while quoting my favorite movies and keeping up with socials? It made life complicated but interesting.

"This sequence and Emma Jean's thoughts don't feel right," I tried to explain as I scowled at the script for the latest movie I was starring in.

Of course, most of the script was dialogue with notes for me so I could stay in Emma Jean's headspace. But I liked to mentally put myself in her shoes, to pretend like I really was Emma Jean on her final day. It was called getting into character. I needed to do that if I was going to sell this role.

Jackson gave me another look.

I began pacing as I tried to figure out how to explain myself.

"Emma Jean Gibbons wouldn't have wanted to take her own life," I said. "She was going to reinvent herself."

"You and I both know that just because someone appears to have everything going for them doesn't mean they really do. Besides, sometimes people reach the top and find it a pretty lonely and sad place to be."

I heard him, but I didn't *hear* him.

I mean, I understood what Jackson was saying. But that didn't change my opinion on the situation.

I continued pacing the kitchen, our Australian shepherd, Ripley, watching my every step as he sat upright between me and Jackson.

"Everything is just too perfect," I continued. "But the thing that really makes me wonder about all of this is the fact that Emma Jean's suicide note was found in the marsh. It wasn't wet or damaged, *and* it was typed."

"You think someone knew she would be riding her bike at that specific time and place and ambushed her. Killed her. Had a forged suicide note with them, and then dropped it beside her body so no one would suspect anything?"

I knew he was saying it so it would sound ludicrous. But it didn't.

Not to me.

I placed my hands on my hips. "Yes, that's exactly what I'm saying."

Jackson stared at me over the top of his "Basically a Detective," coffee mug. I'd given it to him myself, mostly because it amused me to see an actual detective drinking from it. He took the gift in stride, which was just one more thing I loved about him.

"All the evidence points to the fact that her death was a tragic accident," Jackson said. "If she was on the verge of taking her own life, she probably wasn't being careful. According to the script, she was crying. Her tears and the rain probably blinded her. Maybe it was a self-fulfilling prophecy. But the case is closed."

"And why was she riding her bike at night in the middle of nowhere?" I barely heard him.

"Because she was on her way to take her own life."

"I don't buy it. No one thought she was suicidal leading up to her death."

"Are you sure you aren't just seeing crime everywhere?" Jackson propped his hip against the kitchen counter as he studied me. "You do tend to do that. You see neighbors with a rolled-up carpet after hours and assume a body is inside. Or someone suddenly has a lot of money, and you think they got it nefariously. Or—"

"In my defense, sometimes something suspicious *is* going on." I got the point. He didn't need to continue.

"Sometimes?" He gave me a pointed look.

I shook my head. "I'm not exaggerating this time. I'm not."

"What exactly are you planning?"

I paused and looked at him. "What makes you think I'm planning something?"

"Because I know you."

Darn it! He really *did* know me.

Because I *was* making plans. Plans he wouldn't approve of. Plans he wouldn't like. Plans he wouldn't want posted on the newsfeed of his mind.

I knew I needed to change tactics before I got a lecture.

"I'm just thinking maybe I need to get into Emma Jean's head more so I can understand how best to honor her memory." That sounded reasonable—and just like something Jackson would approve of.

He let out a skeptical *uh huh*.

"What? People don't call me an actress for no reason."

I mean, I really *was* an actress. I'd even won a People's Choice Award. *People* magazine had named me one of the fifty most beautiful women—in the entire world. I starred in a hit series, *Relentless*. I'd even done voice-overs for Disney.

"I have a bad feeling about this." Jackson set his coffee on the counter and straightened to his full six-plus feet.

"I have no idea what you might be talking about. I'm just doing what I do." I placed my hand over my heart in a very Scarlett O'Hara pose—Scarlett, the ulti-mate poser.

"You mean, being a very curious actress with a penchant for trouble?" He tilted his head.

I batted my eyelashes innocently and used my best Southern *Gone with the Wind* accent. "Well, frankly, my dear, I am the most boring person you'll ever meet."

"Said no one ever." Jackson kissed my cheek before taking a step back and glancing at his watch. "I've got to get going. You sure you're okay handling things at the rental house while I'm gone?"

Hearing him mention the rental house snapped me from my *Gone with the Wind* thoughts. Several months ago, we'd put Jackson's former residence on the vacation rental market. Normally, Jackson handled things on that front—as if he didn't already have his hands full, mostly with me.

But with him being gone for the week, I'd be in charge. Easy peasy, lemon squeezy. That was what I told myself.

"I'll be fine," I insisted.

"Are you sure? Because I can get Detective Sono to take care of it." Detective Sono was one of Jackson's colleagues at the police station, a good friend, and his sheer size intimidated many—but not everyone.

I waved a hand in the air like I just didn't care. I really needed to prove to both Jackson and myself that I was capable of handling things. "It will be a piece of cake."

"What kind of cake?"

"Not the kind that's baked with a nail file in the center of it." I winked.

That skeptical, although humored, look remained in his eyes. He finally nodded. "You stay out of that said trouble we just talked about."

"I will. I'm going to work on my movie today. That's it."

The low-key grunt made it clear he knew I was up to more than that.

Because I was.

Why would Emma Jean Gibbons want to take her life, especially when she'd just been offered a new record deal and while she had a mysterious man on the side?

All I kept thinking was . . . she wouldn't.

Then how did I explain the suicide note?

I wasn't sure. Maybe she'd been forced to sign it.

But everyone believed she wrote the note, picked up some anti-anxiety pills, and headed to the water on her bicycle to end her life. On the way—in the dark, I might add—she hit a rock, lost her balance, struck her head, and fell into the marsh water.

It all seemed so unlikely.

I mean, why stumble around on a bike on a lonely road after dark?

I had to let this go. Memorize my lines. Rehearse before filming began.

But I knew that was *not* going to happen.

When my curiosity kicked in, everything else needed to get out of the way because my inquisitiveness would race full speed ahead.

I only hoped my quest to find answers didn't end with a crash . . . kind of like Emma Jean's life.

I couldn't stop thinking about Emma Jean's death as I drove to the rental house. As much as I wanted to take a deep dive into the events surrounding it, I needed to do a few things first.

For starters, I needed to deal with a plumbing problem. The renter had texted and was having some issues with the hot water. I totally got that.

Cold showers? No thank you.

I Googled some information so I could sound smart when I arrived. If I knew the right terms to use, I could sell myself as an expert.

I considered it practice as an actress: tapping into skills I was clueless about.

Later, I had to do a second read-through for *Ragdoll*, the new biopic on Emma Jean. "Ragdoll" was the name of one of her songs, though it wasn't the most popular. That would be "Acting on Impulse."

The catchy little ditty began playing in my head.

Let's do this.
Why not?
Got myself in trouble.
Getting help on the double.

Emma Jean Gibbons was a pop country singer who exploded on the scene with her song "Acting on

Impulse." The well-liked tune had been played in commercials, in movies, and all over social media.

She'd released two albums. The second had been an utter failure, and she never managed to regain the popularity she'd achieved at the starting gate. However, with a new contract on the horizon and a secret man in her life, maybe things would have changed for her. Maybe she could have regained some of her momentum.

She originally hailed from Manteo, North Carolina, which was part of the Outer Banks. She'd returned to the area six months before she died.

The five years she'd been in the limelight had taken a toll on her. The sweet, small-town girl was gone, replaced with a world-weary, washed-up singer who didn't know what to do with herself. She'd numbed her sorrows with drugs, alcohol, and men.

That had been so close to being me.

I was so thankful it wasn't.

I'd left Hollywood and had found a simple, normal life here on the shores of the Atlantic Ocean. Though I was still acting, I was much more grounded now.

In the process, I'd found the love of my life, discovered a great group of friends, got myself straight with God, and I felt like a whole new person.

A *better* person.

Coming back down to reality, I stared at the road

in front of me. I'd offered to let the cast come to my place at noon. I'd already arranged for Oh Buoy, a local restaurant specializing in smoothies and sandwiches, to cater lunch for us. I just needed to be back in time to set everything up.

This week, I'd study the script and do the preproduction types of things. Depending on how things went, we might even start filming.

Part of me was excited to dive into another project. It had been a month since *Relentless* finished filming its newest season. We'd ended just in time to celebrate Christmas.

Now it was January, a new year with new projects.

I pulled up to the rental house and paused. The thirteen-hundred-square-foot abode stood on stilts and looked like the quintessential beach house with its cedar siding and nautical decorations—mainly colorful old buoys that hung from various posts.

The front door was open.

Strange. It was winter and in the forties. Why would someone leave the door open when it was so chilly outside?

I wasn't sure, but I felt certain this would mean a higher electric bill.

People didn't exactly call me frugal. But there were some things I put my foot down about. Other people wasting my money was one of them.

I sighed. I might as well just get this over with.

I climbed from my red Miata and walked up the steps to the front door. There was no storm door here, so I peered right inside. "Hello?"

No answer.

"This is Joey," I continued. "I'm here to look at the water heater and see if I can fix it."

I sounded quite confident about my skill level, if I did say so myself. I needed to prove that I could handle these things.

And maybe prove that to Jackson also—not that he'd put me up to the task.

It wasn't that Jackson thought I was spoiled or above doing things like housework or yardwork.

But I *did* like to hire things out a little too much. And order takeout. And I really hated cleaning my house.

When you put that all together, it made me seem prissy. But I wasn't.

I was just a normal girl who happened to star in movies.

Now I just needed to prove the part about me being a normal girl.

When there was still no answer, I took two steps inside—mostly because the cold breeze went right through my clothes and I wanted the walls to block it.

Had the wind blown the door open?

I supposed it was a possibility. The breeze was strong, but I wasn't sure it was *that* strong.

I stopped in my tracks when I saw the dining table in front of me.

There were two place settings at the table, done to the max. There were placemats, linen napkins, plates stacked neatly on top of each other, and silverware arranged in the right pecking order. Two lit candles cast a warm glow on the dozen red roses sitting on the table, and soft music played from somewhere in the background.

It seemed like a weird time of the day to set up a romantic dinner.

Especially since no one appeared to be here, even though there was a car parked in the driveway.

I glanced down the hallway toward the bedrooms.

What if my renter was here, and he or she hadn't realized the front door was open?

This could turn into a very awkward situation.

I took a step back when I noticed a box of Izzes on the kitchen counter.

Izzes . . . one of my favorite drinks. I knew I wasn't the only one who liked them, but it still seemed strange to see them here.

Coincidental, I was sure.

I quickly texted the renter.

Hey, this is the owner of your vacation rental. I'm here to look at the water heater. Are you around?

I waited several minutes with no response.

I started to take a step back when a footstep sounded behind me. A shadow filled the doorway.

Worst-case scenarios were something I lived with daily, like some people lived with stinky feet.

Memories of all the trouble I'd gotten myself into in the past filled my thoughts.

Memories of almost losing my life.

Memories of the enemies I'd made. The obsessive fans. The people with murderous looks in their eyes.

Fear wrapped its tight, claw-like fingers around my throat and squeezed until I could hardly breathe.

chapter
two

"DIDN'T MEAN TO SCARE YOU," a scratchy voice said.

I twirled around and saw . . . Florine Robinson standing there. Jackson's old neighbor. Neighborhood busybody.

The woman had a poof of white hair, a hunched build, and loved wearing floral moo-moos—even when it was cold outside. She walked with a cane and insisted on living by herself.

But despite her physical ailments, the woman was still as sharp as a review from a miserable movie critic.

"I stopped by to check out something for a renter, but it appears no one is here." I frowned to add to the effect of my statement. "Have you seen anyone staying here since he or she arrived?"

My curiosity about whoever was staying here grew.

I let Jackson handle that side of things, so I had no idea who was supposed to be here this week. I only knew a text had been sent to me.

"I can't say I've seen anyone over here. I mean, I'm sure I have at some point, but I haven't really been paying that much attention. There's a Hallmark movie marathon on. That Andrew Walker is so handsome. If only I were young again . . ."

"I see."

But I didn't. Not really. It was all very strange.

My first thought was to call Jackson. But then he might think I couldn't handle it.

That was the last thing I wanted. So maybe I'd simply blow out the candles, lock up, and leave. Then I'd wait to hear from the renter.

But I couldn't just leave Ms. Robinson standing in the doorway.

"Anything in particular that brings you by?" I asked the older woman.

"I was hoping you might help me reach something in one of my cabinets. I'm a little too short, and the doctor doesn't want me climbing up on stools anymore because my bones are as brittle as a thin sheet of ice."

I quickly glanced at the time. I had two hours until the read-through—though I would have helped her even if it meant being a few minutes late.

"Of course I can help you," I told her. "Let me just secure everything here first."

"I'll meet you over there, dear."

Ms. Robinson was the definition of grandmotherly. I wasn't exactly sure how old she was, only that I would label her as elderly.

I blew out the candles and was about to leave when I paused one more time. As I glanced at those Izzes, my gaze wandered to a couple of objects stashed behind the box of drinks.

A roll of trash bags and a small coil of rope.

My throat tightened.

The trash bags could be innocent, right? And the rope . . . maybe whoever was staying here wanted to try his hand at macramé. Or take up climbing . . . though I wasn't sure where he would do that around here. Or . . . . I was sure there were other things people did with rope.

Not every rope was used to tie someone up before torturing and killing them.

Not every trash bag was meant to hide dead body parts.

I wasn't sure why I had such a bad feeling about this. Was it because I happened to see crime around every corner?

Quite possibly.

Or maybe it was because for years I'd dealt with a group that called themselves the Super Stalker Fan Club. They'd had secret online forums, where members shared personal details about my life such as my whereabouts and friends.

Some in the group had been slightly obsessive but innocent. But others had more nefarious intentions.

Though I hadn't heard from the group in a while, I hadn't forgotten about them either.

Whatever this feeling was, I didn't want to stay in this house any longer.

I darted outside, closing and locking the door behind me.

Then I hurried to Ms. Robinson's house so I could grab whatever she wanted from her top shelf and get out of there.

I tried to shake off the bad vibes I'd felt . . . but the task seemed impossible.

"What do you mean this isn't the way it happened?" Selby Lewis, the director of the movie, stared at me as we all sat in my living room.

The man—a fortysomething with plastic-framed

glasses, a tweed jacket, and thinning hair—was intensely serious, like he always had profound—dare I say esoteric?—thoughts.

He'd won two Academy Awards, one for *Love Enchanted*, an epic romance, and another for *Down into the Deep*, a sci-fi thriller.

I'd never worked with him before, but I'd heard good things about him. However, I'd been warned to give him space and that he hated surprises.

If I wanted him to like me, I should try to be laid-back. That was practically my middle name.

I reminded myself to remain calm. To go with the flow.

But it wasn't so easy.

He wasn't the only one staring at me. Everyone's eyes were on me.

All twelve people in the room.

Nine actors who represented real people who had played a part in Emma Jean's life. This wasn't the entire cast, only the people who'd be in certain scenes, along with the director, assistant director, and the writer, a man named Bryant James.

Bryant was a former journalist who'd written the unauthorized biography on Emma Jean.

I'd read it, and, yes, it had been scandalous and sad. And a bestseller.

No one in the book had truly been painted in a positive light.

I repeated for Selby what I'd told Jackson earlier. Something didn't add up about Emma Jean's death.

And I pretty much got the same response from Selby and everyone else in the room as I did from Jackson.

They all looked at me like I was as crazy as a headless chicken.

But I stood behind my theory. The events of Emma Jean's last day didn't ring true with me. There was no way she'd fallen and that note had mysteriously flown out of her pocket and landed in the marsh. If it had been in her pocket, it would have been immersed in the water and unreadable.

Why couldn't anyone else see that?

"Alrighty then . . ." Selby cleared his throat as he stood in front of the group and turned away from me. "Now, if we could get back to the read-through . . ."

We'd already gotten through the death scene, so we were almost done.

Simply reciting the script wasn't entirely too time-consuming, especially considering this movie would only last approximately two hours.

But I had to force myself to concentrate and stop trying to think up theories about what might have actually happened.

Really, it was silly to try and guess.

That meant I needed to investigate. Otherwise, people watching the movie would be able to sense my doubt. I wouldn't be able to truly sell the role I was playing.

We wrapped up the read-through, and I lingered in my kitchen, giving away the leftover food and chatting with the other actors.

Three other "big names" were in the film, which thrilled me. The only thing that would make it better was if Jessica Alba starred in it also.

We'd done a movie together once. We played sisters that were competing spies, but we didn't know each other was a spy. Ever since then, she was my unofficial rival—it was all playful, good-natured fun between us.

I'd been asked to take on this role in *Ragdoll* when the original actress dropped out. Selby had called me personally and asked me.

I'd talked to Jackson and then said yes.

Now, I was working with Richard Watson, Maggie O'Peters, and Flinn McDonnell.

A-Listers.

And they were all in my house right now.

Reading the script and playing with Ripley.

It seemed surreal.

But honestly, they were all more friendly than

some of the newbies who thought they *should* be A-listers.

I chatted with everyone several minutes, taking the opportunity to show off my new parlor trick: lip-syncing. I'd had to learn the ability so I could "sing" Emma Jean's songs. It had taken months of coaching to learn how to act like a pop country star.

To practice, I often tried to move my lips along with people as they talked, seeing if I could copy their motions and expressions.

I did that behind Selby as he told a story and got some laughs.

I was usually good for that.

However, Selby didn't seem amused.

It didn't matter because, in the middle of my soliloquy, someone pounded on my front door.

"I know you're in there!" a female yelled. "And I know what you're doing. You have my permission to make this movie like Ted Bundy gave police the okay to lock him up! Do you understand?"

My eyes widened, and I glanced at Selby.

He narrowed his eyes and let out a puff of air. "That's Kitty Gibbons."

"Emma Jean's mom?" I clarified.

He nodded. "She's been trying to prevent the production of this movie ever since it was announced. She promised she'd do whatever it takes to stop us."

I didn't like the sound of that.

Wherever I was, drama seemed to follow.

Was it me? Or was it life?

I thought I knew the answer, but I wasn't willing to accept the truth.

chapter
three

SELBY FINALLY LET out a resigned sigh and made his way toward the door. I followed behind him.

How had this woman even found out where my house was? And how had she known the cast and crew were meeting here?

Selby opened the door, and I was surprised to see the woman on the other side.

I wasn't sure why I'd expected to see someone older or more bedraggled.

But this woman standing there was the spitting image of Emma Jean, only eighteen years older.

She had the same curly blonde hair that nearly reached her waist. The same big eyes. The same way with words—only Emma Jean had used her gift to create songs people enjoyed whereas Kitty used her words to very colorfully cut other people down.

The woman wasn't crying, nor did she have tissues in her hand.

Instead, she looked angry.

"This isn't your story to tell!" she started as soon as she saw Selby. Then she saw me, and her eyes narrowed even more. "And I can't believe someone like you would associate yourself with a movie like this. You should be ashamed of yourself. It's unauthorized, I'm telling you."

Everyone went quiet behind us. I couldn't blame them. I'd do the same thing in their shoes.

"Now, Mrs. Gibbons . . ." Selby stepped outside and started to shut the door. But before he could, I slipped out behind him.

I told myself it wasn't because I was nosy. I told myself it was because this was my house. Truthfully, it was a mix of both.

"We're going to do your daughter justice in this movie," Selby insisted.

"I know who wrote the script! That good for nothing Bryant James and his yellow journalism. There's *no way* he did her justice."

Neither Selby nor I mentioned that Bryant was inside and maybe even listening.

"On the contrary, I think you'll be quite pleased." Selby pressed his lips together as if repressing a sigh.

"If you think I'll be pleased, then why haven't you

shown me the script?" Kitty popped a hip out and tilted her head. As she waited for Selby's response, she smacked her chewing gum, occasionally popping a bubble.

Irritation lined Selby's face as his wrinkles deepened before my eyes. "Because Emma Jean was a public figure, and that's not the way things work in Hollywood."

"Well, Hollywood can pour it in a juice box and suck it!"

Oh . . . good one. I'd have to remember that expression.

"I'm sorry, Mrs. Gibbons, but I'm going to have to ask you to leave." Selby pointed to her car in the driveway. "This is private property."

"Private property, my foot! *You're* going to lecture *me* about something private? Meanwhile, you're exploiting my daughter's life story all for your slimy little profits?"

The woman had a point.

I wanted to add something useful to the conversation. But in truth, I had no idea what I could say that would make the situation any better.

I'd heard there was some controversy about the movie and that there was friction between Selby and Kitty.

But never in my wildest dreams did I think that

Kitty would track us down here at my house and confront us.

What a way to start things off . . .

To think we'd be spending the next three months of our lives together working on this movie. Would Kitty be there right along with us? Making every step a struggle?

"If you think you're done with me, you're wrong." Kitty Gibbons gave Selby one more searing look before stepping away.

She climbed into her old, beat-up truck, backed out of my driveway—in the process nearly hitting two people walking on the sidewalk—and then sped away.

I glanced at Selby as we stood near my front door.

"I guess you didn't see that one coming?" I started.

"Between Kitty's uninvited presence and your little theory about Emma Jean's death, I'd say I'm ready for this day to be done." His pensive gaze pierced me.

My theory bothered him that much? I found it interesting, to say the least.

After all, why would he be threatened by my idea?

Why would he feel threatened at all?

It wasn't as if he knew Emma Jean personally. But I'd heard from others that Selby was very particular. That was why he did such a good job with his movies.

That also meant he liked things his way or the highway, as the saying went.

The two of us were going to have a good time working together.

Yes, that was sarcasm.

But right now, we needed to face the rest of the cast. Then I'd let Selby explain exactly what had just happened.

The cast left twenty minutes later. Several of them were getting together for dinner tonight and had invited me.

I knew I should go so I could build good rapport with them.

However, my aunt had asked me to eat with her tonight. I wasn't sure, but I thought she and her on-again, off-again boyfriend might be having problems. He was a painter with an artistic temperament, and Dizzy was used to being on her own.

Even though I briefly considered canceling, I knew I couldn't do that.

Dizzy needed me, and I planned on being there for her.

But I still had a little bit of time before I met her.

I sat down on my couch with my computer, and Ripley jumped beside me, resting his chin on my leg.

As I patted his head, memories of going to the rental house earlier played in my mind.

I hadn't heard back from the renter, which I found odd.

I also thought those items I'd discovered in his house were odd.

My brain was doing all kinds of wacky things—and making wacky assumptions.

I located the spreadsheet Jackson had set up to keep track of who was renting. That was where I found this guy's full name. Ezra Cambridge.

He was thirty-three years old and from Pennsylvania. Based on the paperwork, he'd come to Nags Head alone.

Which made that whole dinner-for-two thing pretty interesting.

Most people who came to the Outer Banks at this time of year weren't here for typical beach vacations. Though there could be warm days, there could also be cold days—like today.

At this time of the year, we occasionally got some fishermen. But mostly it was just people who wanted to get away from things and come to these islands to relax. This area wasn't exactly a dating mecca or anything.

Out of curiosity, I typed Ezra's name into Google.

Quite a few results popped up.

I found the correct Ezra Cambridge from Pennsylvania and clicked on one of his social media profiles.

I frowned at what I read. He worked at home processing claims for an insurance company. He was also a D&D dungeon master, and he liked cosplay.

In his photos, he had an awkward look in his eyes, like he wasn't comfortable in social situations.

His nose was a little too long, his brow a little too dominant, and his skin a little too pale.

Almost like a vampire.

But not the Robert Pattinson kind. More like one of the Munsters.

He also liked Ramen, character socks, and . . . *Relentless*.

Coincidence? Doubted it.

This guy seemed to have a bit of an obsessive personality, if you asked me.

I frowned and rubbed Ripley's head some more.

I'd give Ezra another hour or two to get back with me then I'd try to contact him again.

After all, what if something was wrong?

But for right now, I needed to get ready for dinner with Dizzy.

DIZZY JENKINS and I sat across from each other at Meatsa Eatsa, my favorite burger joint in the area. We'd already ordered our favs, and now we munched on some onion rings while we waited for the main course.

Dizzy was my aunt and a hairdresser. In fact, I'd worked with her for a while when I'd moved back to this area as I tried to figure my life out.

Her husband—my dad's brother—had died several years ago, and now she filled her days with her friends, working, and shenanigans.

She was in her sixties with dyed dark hair that she piled on top of her head. Her trademark blue eyeshadow went from her lashes to her brow, and she had no shame in it.

I'd always liked people who didn't care what other people thought. That was Dizzy.

She'd started dating Wesley, a painter, a while ago, and they'd been on-again, off-again since then.

But her angst tonight was because Wesley wasn't paying her enough attention. Did that mean he was losing interest? Was the end in sight?

Those were Dizzy's worries.

That or maybe he'd dumped her for a super model.

The last thing I could imagine was a super model going for someone like Wesley, but . . .

I'd quickly assured her that he was probably fine and maybe they should simply talk about it. Conversations could be an amazing resource to find out how people truly felt.

I knew it because I'd been there before.

And I was sure I'd be there again.

Either way, it turned out my fears about her man problems were overblown.

Dizzy wiped her lips with a napkin before placing the cloth back in her lap. "Now, enough about me. What's going on with you?"

Where did I start?

Before I could, our food was delivered, and we lifted a prayer.

As soon as I said amen, Dizzy charged ahead, not waiting for me to answer her earlier question. "Did you open the envelope yet? I'm sorry—I just have to know, though. I've been thinking about it for a while and waiting for you to bring the subject up. But you haven't."

She stared at me, a motherly kind of nurturing look in her eyes.

Without asking for clarification, I knew exactly what she was talking about.

Tension stretched across my chest, and the act of breathing suddenly felt unnatural, like something I had to force myself to do.

This past summer, a man named Adolf Casperson had come forward and claimed to be my real father. He'd said he had an affair with my mother right before she met and quickly married my father.

Currently, my mother was in the wind—rumor had it she worked for the CIA—and my dad, the one I'd grown up with, was now in witness protection.

It was messy. Really messy.

But I couldn't ask either of them for the truth. Instead, I'd demanded a DNA test so I could know if Adolf was lying or not.

I'd gotten the results back via the postal service, sealed in an envelope for my eyes only. And . . .

"I still haven't opened it," I admitted.

It had been more than six months now.

A long time. But I knew that whatever was inside

that envelope could change my life, and I wasn't sure I was ready for that.

So instead, I procrastinated.

Jackson had encouraged me to open it at first, but he'd finally given me space to process it in my own way.

Apparently, I was still processing.

Meanwhile, Adolf had left the area. On occasion, I got a text from him, but I hadn't seen him since. I'd already told him I was having the DNA test done—he'd given me a sample—and that I wasn't sure when I'd look at the results.

Thankfully, he hadn't pushed.

I hadn't seen my real dad—the dad I'd grown up with—in more than a year.

I missed him terribly, but there were people out there who wanted him dead.

That was all thanks to my mother.

And other people thought that their families were messed up . . .

They didn't know the half of it. My life could be a *Lifetime* movie.

"I'm sure you'll open the results when you're ready," Dizzy finally said. "Now, what else?"

I considered telling her about the creepy renter, but I decided not to. Not yet. Not until I knew more. I planned on either texting or calling Ezra again a bit later.

Instead, I told Dizzy some of the details about the upcoming Emma Jean Gibbons biopic and the events unfolding around it today.

She twisted her neck in a curious manner when I finished. "You don't think Emma Jean wanted to take her own life? You think her death was accidental?"

"I know it sounds silly, but the facts aren't adding up to me. I've been studying this woman's life for the past three months. I've learned her songs. I've read interviews she did. I've watched recorded concerts." I shook my head slowly. "She didn't strike me as someone who'd want to end her life. The fact she died on the way to do so seems too coincidental."

"Well, you know—"

"Yes, I know that not everyone who's suicidal appears to be suicidal. I know that sometimes it's a spur-of-the-moment decision, an impulse, and not something that they've been considering for a long time. But—"

"I was going to say, you know that the pharmacist who was on duty the day she went into the drugstore still works at McCauley's RX?" She stared at me, watching for my reaction. "Glenn Pumpernickel."

I raised my eyebrows. "He does? How do you know that?"

She shrugged. "I cut his hair, of course."

Why hadn't I heard about this before? All these

months of studying Emma Jean's life, and *now* this came up? It seemed like something Dizzy would have mentioned earlier.

"He's an amazing man," Dizzy continued. "His wife died about a year and a half ago from cancer. She fought a long battle. Rumor has it he lost his house trying to pay for her treatments."

"That's terrible."

"It is. But he tries to look on the bright side. Anyway, he loves talking about Emma Jean. He was one of her biggest fans."

"What are you hinting at, Dizzy?" I watched her expression.

She smirked and did a half shrug. "I'm just saying if you ever want to get some more insight into Emma Jean, Glenn might be a good person to talk to."

I stared at Dizzy before slowly nodding. "I like the way you think."

"I thought you might."

"And if I go to talk to this pharmacist, do you want to come with me?"

"Do you think he's still at work?" She glanced at the time. "It's almost six."

"It's worth a shot. So what do you say?"

She grinned. "I thought you'd never ask."

~

As Dizzy and I stood outside of the drugstore, she squealed and clapped. "I'm so excited about solving another crime with you . . ."

I cringed at her words—probably because I'd been around Jackson too much. He was adamantly opposed to me involving myself in any type of criminal investigations, especially if he wasn't there to watch my back.

I nibbled on my lip before saying, "Let's call it character research. It makes Jackson more comfortable when I say it that way."

She gave me a side eye and raised an eyebrow before grinning. "*Character research* it is."

"I'm not saying this 'research' is going to lead anywhere. But something about Emma Jean's death doesn't feel right to me, and I can't just let this go."

"Well, it can't hurt to ask."

That had to be the most untrue statement I'd ever heard. Investigating crimes *could* do a lot of harm. Anyone who knew me could testify to that fact, since I nearly died at least ten times already.

I looked at the drugstore again. The place was in an old strip of shoppes—not shops, as per the sign—in historic Manteo, North Carolina.

The place was the home of Virginia Dare, the first child born to Englishers in what would become the United States.

The place where the historic people of Roanoke Island had disappeared more than four hundred years ago.

McCauley's RX was in a brick-fronted building that had been painted white. It looked as if it was stuck in a different era, back when times were simpler.

I gathered my wits about me as Dizzy and I walked inside. Sometimes people recognized me. But sometimes they didn't. Sometimes that worked to my advantage, and sometimes it didn't.

It was always a shot in the dark.

Dizzy led toward an older gentleman working the pharmacy counter at the back.

Thankfully, I didn't see any other customers nearby.

"Can I help you?" He glanced up at me.

Then he saw Dizzy, and a grin cracked across his otherwise crotchety face. "Dizzy Jenkins. What brings you in here?"

Dizzy giggled. "It's good to see you too. My friend has a couple of questions for you."

He looked back at me, his grin dimming some. "What do you need?"

"Hi, I'm Joey. I'm actually an actress who is playing Emma Jean Gibbons for the upcoming biopic movie on her life."

He didn't look impressed nor show any signs of

recognition. In fact, if anything, he almost appeared like I might be making all of this up.

Not a good sign.

"I understand that Emma Jean came in here the day she died, and I was hoping to talk to someone for research for my role."

He let out a skeptical grunt. "Researching, huh? You sure you're not a journalist trying to get the inside scoop? Had plenty of those come around here."

He continued to sort his medicines.

"She really is playing Emma Jean in the movie," Dizzy backed me up.

Keeping his head low, only his eyes flickered up. "Uh huh."

Dizzy reached over and grabbed a magazine. "If you don't believe us, then look at this." She thrust it at him.

I saw a copy of *Woman's World*. And I was on the front cover, smiling as I talked about my favorite recipes.

As if I cooked.

Jackson had given me a few quick lessons, enough that I could honestly say that, yes, I really did cook—if oatmeal, avocado toast, and smoothies counted.

The man looked from the magazine to me and then back to the magazine again.

Then he paused from what he was doing.

He recognized me now.
Would he help us?
Or would he scoff and turn us down?
To agree or not to agree. That was the question.

chapter
five

"OKAY. MY APOLOGIES." Glenn Pumpernickel pushed his wire-framed glasses up higher on his nose, looking at Dizzy as he said the words. "I guess I get protective. Right after Emma Jean passed, I had numerous people come into my store and try to get information from me. I don't like to be a gossip. Is that why you're here? To hear the scuttlebutt?"

I quickly shook my head. "I'm not here to stir up trouble. I'm just trying to retrace her final steps. Something doesn't feel right to me about the way she died. I'm just trying to put my finger on what."

His gaze softened. "I think we were all shocked when we learned she'd died—especially in that manner. None of us could believe it."

"So you knew her before she got famous?" I asked.

"I did. Went to church with her and her mom.

Grew up listening to her singing 'Amazing Grace' on Sunday mornings and Leanne Rimes and Taylor Swift songs at the local fairs."

"Talk about down-home." I was trying to establish some rapport with this guy, and I thought it was working.

"I always tried to support her however I could," he continued. "Sometimes she didn't have money to travel to fairs or enter contests. I would try to slip them some cash as a way of showing my support. Emma Jean was always appreciative."

"I bet."

"That girl was so sweet . . . until fame got to her. It messed her up." He shook his head and frowned before absently beginning to sort some paper bags on the counter.

I'd heard *that* story before.

In fact, I had lived that story before.

"Did you talk to her when she came in that day?" I tried to sound gentle and not spook the man—because I had a feeling he could be easily spooked.

"I did. I still remember it pretty vividly. I could tell something was wrong, but she didn't want to talk. She just said it had been a long day and that she had a headache."

I nodded as I pictured it playing out. "Then she paid for her medicine and left?"

"That's right. I hoped that with some rest she'd be fine."

"Was there anything strange about her being in here?" I asked. "Was she alone? Did she say anything weird?"

Glenn thought about it a moment, pressing his lips together in a grim line. "I've replayed her visit here a million times. No, she didn't say anything suspicious. But . . ."

Dizzy and I both leaned closer.

"Yes?" I asked.

He clucked his tongue and shook his head again as if brushing off the thought. "It was probably nothing."

"What was probably nothing?" I could hardly breathe as I waited for him to continue.

"I couldn't help but notice a man lingering at the back of the store. He kept glancing at Emma Jean as she talked to me. I thought maybe he was a fan."

"So he wasn't someone you recognized?" Dizzy asked.

He shook his head. "No, I'd never seen him before. Although I have to say I didn't truly get a good look at him. He was pretty far away."

"Was there anything about him that made you suspicious?" I asked.

"There was something about the way he looked at her *and* the way Emma Jean kept looking in this security mirror." He pointed to a round reflector perched in the corner, one that allowed the person working behind the counter to see anything happening out of eyesight.

"So maybe this guy was making her nervous too." I pursed my lips as I processed that.

"I suspect he was. I even asked Emma Jean if she wanted me to walk her out. But she laughed it off and said she was fine."

Maybe I *was* onto something.

And maybe my idea wasn't as crazy as it sounded.

"You should try to talk to Bobbi or Maverick also," Glenn continued.

Bobbi Sawyer had been Emma Jean's high school best friend, and Maverick Price had been Emma Jean's high school boyfriend.

"They're on my list," I told him. "They still around here?"

"Last I heard. Bobbi does private music lessons, and Maverick does something with his boat." Glenn paused and shifted. "I actually still have some video footage from that day."

My eyes widened, and then I blinked, unsure I'd heard correctly. "You do?"

I hadn't expected that.

"I saved it. I tried to give it to the police, but they didn't seem interested. Didn't really consider her death to be criminal, if you know what I mean. But I always wondered if her death would come back up one day. Like right now."

"Any chance we could see it?"

"I made multiple copies. I'll give you one. I've never felt like everything was right with her death. If you guys are looking into it as a part of this movie that you're making . . . then go for it. I'd love to shine some light on what really happened . . . if anybody can figure that out." He crossed his arms as if issuing a challenge to me.

My heart raced faster.

That had been easy.

Maybe even too easy.

I ran into my first problem when I realized that Glenn was giving me this video footage on a DVD.

I had gotten rid of my DVD player a while ago. I might be able to find one somewhere, but this wasn't ideal.

Glenn was gracious and allowed us to watch the video on a small TV in the employees only room in the back. The place smelled like microwaved meals and a toilet that hadn't been flushed.

Dizzy and I ignored that as we sat at an old table on

rickety chairs. We leaned close to the TV so we wouldn't miss any details. But the footage was grainy at best.

The security camera angle was right above the pharmacy counter.

As clear as day, I saw Emma Jean come in.

The woman was beautiful with a winning smile. But as I watched her walk up to the pharmacy counter, I realized her gaze told the real story. She looked anything but happy.

Maybe she truly was distraught that day.

Distraught enough to take her own life?

I had no idea.

My gaze wandered to the back of the screen.

A man lingered nearly out of sight of the camera. He was tall with dark hair and a brooding gaze. Part of his face was concealed by some kind of display at the end of the aisle. All I could make out was that he seemed to be watching Emma Jean.

Based on the way Emma Jean glanced back at him, she clearly knew he was there. Maybe he even made her nervous. After all, her gaze seemed shaky, and she kept playing with her hair.

But who was that guy?

"I don't suppose you recognize him, do you?" I turned to Dizzy.

As she stared at his image, I grabbed my phone and

took a picture of the video footage. Maybe I could blow it up and enhance the image. But I doubted it.

Dizzy had lived in the area for as long as I could remember, so I knew there was a slight chance she'd recognize him.

Dizzy shrugged and shook her head. "Can't say he's familiar."

"If he's not a local, then it's going to be difficult to ID him."

"You're trying to figure out who that guy is?" someone asked behind us.

I perked as I turned.

The cashier—the one who looked like she was in high school—stood there. She had stringy blonde hair, a smattering of acne on her cheeks, and braces.

Those high school years could be awkward for some people. I'd been one of them, so there was no judgment from me.

"We are," I said. "You don't know him by chance, do you?"

She leaned closer to study the image more. "I think his name is Todd. He works over at Rusty's Auto Service."

Okay . . . I'd wanted easy, and it appeared that was exactly what I'd gotten.

Things *never* worked out that way.

Well, usually never.

I lifted up a prayer of thanks.

"What's your name?" I asked.

"Julie."

"Thanks for the information, Julie. Has Todd lived here long?"

"I think he's been here in the area for about ten years now. He went to high school with my brother."

"So why didn't Glenn know him?" Dizzy asked.

Good question. It just seemed odd that this girl would know him, but the pharmacist didn't.

"Rusty's Auto Service isn't exactly the kind of place that Mr. Pumpernickel takes his vehicles. And if people don't go to church with him or come into the pharmacy then Mr. Pumpernickel wouldn't know them."

I supposed I could see that. The town was small, but maybe not *that* small. Last I heard, just under two thousand people lived in Manteo. I'd looked up that fact when doing my research for the movie.

"Rusty's Auto Service?" I repeated.

"That's right. It's about a mile down the road. If I had to guess, it probably closed about thirty minutes ago, however." Julie squinted and stared at the screen. "What's that from anyway?"

I quickly turned the TV off. The last thing I needed to do was to start rumors. "Nothing important. Just doing some research for a role in a new movie."

Her eyes widened. "You're Joey Darling, aren't you? I thought you looked familiar!"

"That's me . . ."

"You're a little heavier in real life, though. Shorter too."

Heavier? My lips parted in shock. What?

I glanced down at my hips, resenting that comment. Before I could respond, Julie continued. I shoved the offense aside—for now.

"I love *Relentless*," she gushed. "My friends and I have viewing parties to watch it every week."

"That's awesome." I flashed a smile, trying to ignore her earlier insult. "I really appreciate your help."

Then Dizzy and I stood and said goodbye before quickly hurrying out the door.

I kept the DVD just in case I needed it later. If push came to shove, I *would* find a DVD player so I could watch this again. I'd buy one off eBay if I had to. If that failed, I'd go to the dump myself and search through the land of forgotten electronics from bygone eras.

The things I'd do for research . . . there were really no limits.

chapter
six

DIZZY and I swung by Rusty's, but it was closed, just as I expected.

Now that winter hours were upon us, darkness had already fallen outside. It felt like midnight when, in actuality, it was only six-thirty.

I dropped Dizzy off at her car, promised to keep her updated, and then headed back to my house.

Until I decided *not* to head back to my house.

Ezra still hadn't called me back or replied to my text.

Part of me wanted to let this go, to not be overbearing. This man's vacation was none of my business.

But I was concerned.

And to be completely honest, I was also curious.

The responsible thing to do was to swing by the place and make sure everything was okay.

So that was what I did.

When I pulled up, the house looked just as it had earlier.

A beat-up black sedan was parked beneath it, and the front door was open . . . again.

I pressed my lips together. Did Ezra just want to drive up my heating costs?

The old Joey wouldn't have thought much about that. In fact, it was still throwing me for a loop that I even cared about energy costs.

But the switch in my personality wasn't my biggest concern at the moment.

Why was that door open . . . again? If the guy wanted some air, why not open a window or the sliding patio door instead?

I stared at the house, hesitating to get out of my car.

What if something was wrong inside?

It's probably nothing, I told myself. *Your imagination is just going crazy right now.*

With that thought, I let out a long sigh then grabbed the door handle.

I stepped out, stared at that front door one more time, and then started up the wooden steps leading to the deck.

Just to be on the safe side, I had my cell phone handy in case I needed to call backup.

The closer I got to the top of the stairs, the slower my steps became.

Finally, I paused near the door and peered inside. "Hello?"

No answer.

But as I looked through the doorway, I spotted those glowing candles on the dining room table again.

Except this time, they were half melted. That meant they'd been burning a while and were a fire hazard.

Fire hazard? Here I went again thinking like a responsible homeowner. Joey Darling was growing up.

I could *not* let our rental burn down this week while Jackson was gone.

Not only would he be devastated, but I'd feel like it was my fault, that I'd failed.

I couldn't let that happen.

Joey Darling Sullivan was *not* going to fail.

But I still didn't move.

This whole situation was strange.

Maybe I should call one of Jackson's colleagues.

Or maybe I was just overthinking this again.

There was nothing dangerous about a romantic candlelight dinner for . . . no one.

A dinner for no one because my renter had disappeared.

But someone had clearly come back after I left

earlier today to light these candles again and leave the door open.

I remembered the items I'd seen earlier. The Izzes. The trash bags. The rope.

I hesitated.

Step inside and blow out the candles?

Or just leave?

Those were my options.

I just needed to bite the bullet and blow out those candles. Then I'd leave and be on my merry way. I wouldn't worry about this anymore because it wasn't my business.

Except maybe it was.

I mean, Jackson and I owned this house. It was officially our business. But that didn't mean I needed to police the actions of those inside. I wasn't the guardian of everyone who rented the place.

I needed to know my boundaries.

That was what my counselor used to tell me when I'd gone through my divorce. She'd been right on the money. Boundaries didn't help others in my life. Boundaries were for me to set limits and protect my sanity.

I stepped inside, trying to ignore the tremble quaking through my hands.

Who could blame me? It had been one of those days—starting when Kitty Gibbons had shown up at my house with her mama-bear claws out.

How many other people in this area were angry because of the biopic? Would any of those people be mad at me?

In my experience, I'd say the answer was yes.

I'd met a lot of really kooky people in my days as an actress.

People who wanted to be me.

People who wanted to worship me.

People who hated me for being me.

Life wasn't exactly simple, especially when the public was easily triggered, offended, and obsessed. I knew it came with the territory, but that didn't mean it wasn't frustrating.

I rushed toward the candles, determined to get this over with.

Reaching them, I carefully blew out the flames.

Then stepped back ready to flee.

As I did, I hit something.

Something that hadn't been there only seconds ago.

Or should I say, *someone* who hadn't been there only seconds ago.

chapter
seven

I **GASPED** as I turned around.

Ezra Cambridge stood there.

And he looked even more socially awkward in person than he did on social media.

His mustache was a little too long and shaggy over his front lip. His hair was thinning yet too long. His face too pale. His body too thin.

Definite vampire vibes.

"I didn't mean to scare you," he started, his gaze strangely transfixed on me.

Something about his words brought me back down to earth. "I guess I shouldn't have come inside. But I called, and no one answered. I was worried. Did you get my text or phone call earlier?"

"Phone's dead." He shrugged nonchalantly. "Figured it was better to go electronic-free while I was here anyway."

Hmm. That was odd.

He had texted me—on an electronic device—about the hot water issue.

I swallowed hard, trying not to overthink this situation. "I stopped by earlier because you said something about the water heater."

He stared at me a little too hard. A little too unblinking.

Didn't normal people glance away in the course of a conversation?

Not Ezra. His gaze was intense and persistent—almost like a vampire wanting to suck some blood.

"The water heater started working again," he said. "I guess I should have tried to let you know somehow."

I thought about bringing up the fact he'd used a cell phone here already, but figured I might not want to push any of this guy's buttons.

"I stopped by earlier, but you weren't here," I told him, curious about that whole situation.

"I must have been in the bathroom. I didn't hear you."

Why did I doubt that?

Instead, I nodded, a little too quickly, too stiffly.

"I'm so glad that worked out." I pointed behind

him. "I guess I'll be going. Didn't mean to interrupt anything."

As I tried to step by Ezra, he subtly moved in front of me, blocking my path.

I could probably push past him if I had to. But I didn't want to overreact. Not yet.

"This is a great house." He stared down at me, clearly trying to extend our conversation. "I'm so glad I found it online."

"Jackson and I like it." I was careful to mention my husband's name just to make sure this guy knew I was married—in case he was thinking about hitting on me or anything.

Not that a wedding ring stopped that anymore.

"You're a great actress. You probably already know that." Ezra let out a self-conscious laugh.

"I appreciate that." Sweat began to trickle down my back.

"I can't believe you make house calls yourself. I had no idea."

I rubbed my hands on my jeans, noticing that my palms were also sweaty. "I don't always make house calls. But I made an exception today."

I didn't dare tell him that Jackson was out of town.

I pointed at that table for two one more time. "I really should go so you can enjoy your dinner."

Ezra didn't bother to look at the table. His gaze remained on me. "It's no hurry."

I glanced at my watch. "I wish I could say the same. Unfortunately, I've got a full schedule right now. I've gotta run."

In reality, the only thing I had on my agenda for tonight was relaxing and talking to Jackson. But Ezra didn't know that.

"There's no need to rush away."

I slipped by him. Once I reached the deck, I breathed a little easier. But I knew I wouldn't relax until I was in my car with the doors locked.

"Have a great stay here on the Outer Banks," I called over my shoulder.

I hurried down to my car, climbed in, and locked the doors.

But even as I pulled away, I glanced up and noticed that Ezra Cambridge was still standing in his doorway, watching me leave. His still dark silhouette almost reminded me of a bat . . . watching its prey before attacking.

I really shouldn't have done that *Twilight* movie marathon a couple of weeks ago . . .

A shudder captured me as I hightailed it out of there.

~

I was still shaking when I got back to my house.

Ripley greeted me at the door as I quickly slipped inside and twisted the lock in place behind me.

Not that I thought that Ezra had followed me.

The truth was, Ezra might be an okay guy. Just because he was socially awkward and looked like a vampire didn't mean he was dangerous or that there was anything wrong with him.

But past experience had taught me to be on guard. Something about the interaction I'd had with him didn't sit right with me.

All I wanted to do right now was to call Jackson.

It was past eight p.m., so he should be finished with his training for the day.

Even though we'd only been married less than a year, I'd quickly gotten used to living with him. Up until this moment, I didn't realize how much I looked forward to having him and Ripley here to greet me when I came home.

When I'd been down in Wilmington filming *Relentless*, it had been nice to come home on the weekends. But it was rare for me to be here in this house without Jackson.

I didn't like it.

I took several deep breaths before stepping toward the kitchen.

I gripped my purse as I glanced around. I couldn't help but wonder if more danger lurked close.

Maybe not even Ezra.

But maybe Kitty Gibbons.

I set my purse on the counter.

At just that moment, music filled the room.

Not just any music.

Emma Jean's music.

"Ragdoll," to be exact.

I'm disappearing,
Right before your eyes,
There's no way to disguise,
What's become of me.

My blood went ice cold.

What if it was someone worse than Ezra or Kitty?

What if Emma Jean herself had come back to haunt me?

chapter
eight

WAIT . . . was that music coming from . . . my purse?

I quickly grabbed my bag and searched the contents until I found . . . my phone.

Sure enough, a little icon on my home screen showed that one of my music apps had begun playing.

I quickly hit the button and turned it off.

What in the . . . ?

I *had* been listening to Emma Jean's music earlier. Maybe I'd jostled something inside my purse and the music had somehow started playing.

Still, I couldn't shake the eeriness around me.

But if there was a ghost in the house, Ripley would have let me know, right? Dogs had a sense about those things.

Instead of barking and snarling at some unseen

force, Ripley wagged his tail and looked up at me with his adoring eyes.

I had to get a grip.

I reminded myself I didn't believe in ghosts. Or vampires—but that was a different thought for a different time.

But for a moment, I'd almost felt convinced that Emma Jean was seeking revenge on me for being in this movie.

I let out a mental sigh.

I really had to shake this off.

I walked to my pantry and grabbed a bottle of water, drinking half of it as I stood there.

Tomorrow was a busy day, and I needed to get some rest. We were going to begin some of the initial blocking of the scenes. Plus, I needed to meet with makeup and wardrobe.

This movie really was going to start filming.

First, I'd hop in the shower and let the hot water wash away some of my anxiety.

Then I'd call Jackson.

An hour later, I was wearing my favorite PJs and sipping on hot chocolate as I huddled on the couch, Ripley sitting beside me.

My phone rested on the arm of the couch with Jackson on speaker.

"So how did today go?" His deep, rich voice floated through the line, instantly bringing me comfort.

I thought about what to say then decided to delay my update about Emma Jean. I wasn't sure how he'd react.

"Why talk about *me* when we can talk about *you*?" I asked. "After all, what you're doing is much more interesting."

He began telling me about his "Identifying and Handling Critical Situations in High-Risk Environments" training.

"So you avoided my question earlier," he said when he finished. "What happened with you today? You didn't tell other people about your theory concerning Emma Jean's death, did you?"

The memory of me telling the cast replayed in my mind, and I frowned. "You really think I'd do that?"

"I guess that answers that question," he said dryly. "What about the rental house? Everything going okay with that? Were you able to stop by about the water heater?"

"I have it all handled." I didn't bother to tell him about the creepy vampire-like man there. And I wouldn't. Not until I had a real reason to.

Jackson and I chatted a few more minutes before I

told him I loved him, and we got off the phone. I felt better now that I'd talked to him.

I sat for a while longer enjoying the peace and quiet.

Then, before I climbed in bed, I peered out my window.

Someone stood on the sidewalk at the front of the house.

The figure was shadowed so I couldn't make out any features.

Then I saw a small light.

Whoever it was, he'd just lit a cigarette, I realized.

Was that why he'd stopped out front? To light up?

Or was he standing there so he could watch my house?

I dropped the curtain.

I didn't know.

Another part of me didn't want to know.

I hadn't dug deeply enough into anything yet to push anyone's buttons.

But that didn't mean trouble hadn't come calling.

chapter
nine

THANKFULLY, the night was uneventful.

The person I'd seen outside must have been someone on their nightly walk who'd stopped to take a smoke.

Nothing to worry about.

My paranoia was just being paranoid.

Yes, that was a thing.

I had to meet the rest of the cast and crew at one of our shooting locations this morning so we could block some scenes. But I didn't have to be there till nine.

I'd already looked up Rusty's Garage. It opened at eight, so I planned to swing by on my way to the set.

Cue to this moment.

I pulled to a stop in front of the business.

Rusty's was your run-of-the-mill garage, located on what locals called the main drag through town. The building was white with three oversized garage doors out front and uncountable vehicles surrounding the property.

I didn't see any available parking spaces, so I made my own near the front door. Then I strode inside and glanced around.

One of the mechanics saw me and let out a whistle.

"Can I help you, pretty lady?" His voice made him sound like he was trying a little too hard.

"I'm looking for Todd," I told him.

"Todd?" He glanced at one of the mechanics working in the bay. "You didn't tell me you had a new girl."

"I don't." The man—Todd, I assumed—finished doing something beneath a car with a wrench before stepping out. He grabbed a rag from over his shoulder and wiped his greasy hands before heading toward me.

As he got closer, his eyes narrowed as if he recognized me.

I got that reaction a lot.

"Do I know you?" He paused in front of me.

"We've never met," I started. "But I was hoping to ask you a few questions."

"About what?" His voice sounded tense as if he feared I might be an undercover cop or something.

"About Emma Jean Gibbons."

He narrowed his eyes even more—any narrower,

and he wouldn't be able to see me. "Why do you want to know about Emma Jean?"

"I'm actually playing Emma Jean in the new biopic."

Realization rolled over his features. "You're Joey Darling. I *knew* I'd seen you somewhere before."

I wasn't sure if that was a liability or asset right now. "Would you mind talking?"

He didn't say anything a moment. "Normally, I'd say no. But since it's you, I'll talk."

I didn't know what that meant. Was it because I was an actress that he would talk to me? Because I was Joey Darling the actress?

I really had no idea, but I wasn't about to question him.

He pointed to a door leading to the back of the property, and we stepped out.

More cars sat back here, along with a view of the marsh leading to the Roanoke Sound. This property could probably go for a lot of money if the right developer got his or her hands on it. Back when the place had opened, no one had probably thought anything about the future value of waterfront property.

It almost seemed like a waste.

"What do you want to know?" Todd took his rag and began to wipe the grease from his hands again.

The guy seemed nice enough, and I could see

where Emma Jean might have been attracted to him. Was Todd the mystery man that had been referenced before she died?

His build nicely filled out his mechanic's uniform—I noted that as a matter of observation not attraction. He had thick brown hair and a barely there beard and mustache.

I did love barely there beards and mustaches. Jackson had one also.

The thought of it made me miss my Jackson. This was going to be the longest week ever without him here.

I glanced at Todd again. Where did I even start with this guy?

I figured at the beginning was as good a place as any.

"I heard you went to the pharmacy with Emma Jean on the day she died."

He glanced up at the statement. "I did. How did you know that?"

"I saw the video footage. I'm sure the police have already talked to you."

"They have. But I didn't want anyone else to know and start asking questions."

I wasn't sure what kind of sense I was getting about this guy. Part of me wanted to like him because he was the down-home type. But another part of me thought he was acting shifty.

"How did you know her?" I turned away from the wind as it brought with it the putrid scent of the marsh.

He glanced out at the water, seeming nose-blind to the scent. "You won't believe me if I tell you."

"Try me."

His jaw tightened before he said, "After she moved back, she had to bring her car into the shop because of some transmission problems. We started talking and hit it off."

"You're telling me that a hometown boy caught the eye of a big superstar?" I asked the question tongue-in-cheek. "When does *that* ever happen?"

In reality, that was pretty much exactly what my story with Jackson was.

"That's right. I couldn't believe it either."

"So you were her mystery man," I clarified.

He shook his head. "There was never anything between us. We were friends, and I was someone she could talk to. I think she was seeing someone else, but she never told me who. I didn't ask. Maybe part of me didn't want to know."

"Why would she keep this guy a secret? Did you feel like she was leading you on?" Maybe I shouldn't have asked the last part, but I did.

"She made it clear we were just friends, and I respected that." He paused. "I did wonder if maybe we might be something more one day. But we never got that chance." His voice drifted off wistfully.

And I found myself wishing that the two of them had gotten a chance also.

I swallowed hard before continuing to question Todd.

"Did you have any idea that day when you were with Emma Jean that she might try to take her life that night?"

Todd shook his head. "No. And I still don't believe it. She said she'd had a decent morning. She'd been out by the water at her house working on some songs. Everything seemed pretty normal."

"Strange."

"I know. I mean, I knew Emma Jean was going through some things, but there were no indications she was ready to end it all. In fact, there were indications she wanted to make changes. She had a new record deal in the works and was feeling hopeful. She'd even booked a vacation down in the Caribbean, hoping it would inspire her to write some more songs. Why would she go about making these plans if she knew she was going to end things?"

Excellent point.

Why hadn't anyone brought that up before? It seemed like everyone so easily believed she'd wanted to take her own life and had accidentally died on the way to do so.

Were Todd and I the only skeptical ones?

I shifted as I settled in for the conversation. "If you don't mind me asking, what kind of things was she going through?"

"For starters, her manager was overbearing. Her mom was always concerned about money—how much she was owed to be specific. Fans had expectations, and Emma Jean feared disappointing them. Then there were the overzealous devotees."

I could relate to everything he said. In fact, part of me felt like Emma Jean and I could have been friends.

"Overzealous fans? Did anyone threaten her?"

Todd narrowed his eyes. "Wait . . . you think that this was something more too, don't you?"

I shrugged. I didn't want to totally agree with him and get him worked up.

What I was doing was a job or maybe even a hobby, depending on who you asked. But what Todd was dealing with was his heart. I needed to be careful as I treaded forward.

"I'm trying to get into her mind."

"She was acting spooked and irritable. It was weird

because she seemed to be finding some peace. Then the week before she died, everything changed. She seemed so stressed out."

"She never said why?"

"I asked, but she just brushed me off. And she was constantly looking over her shoulder."

Ah ha! More proof that something could have happened.

"Did the pressure ever get to her, or was there something else?" I tried to keep the emotion from my voice.

"Everyone wanted something of her." He stared at me, compassion cracking his words.

I could see why Emma Jean had enjoyed speaking with Todd. He was sympathetic, a good listener, and seemed like a genuinely authentic person.

I licked my lips before asking, "But did anyone want her dead?"

"That's an excellent question. I'd love to know the answer to it. Would love to go back and have one more opportunity to talk to her before . . ." He wiped beneath his eye.

"Often with great love and fame comes great hate and despising. I'm sure she felt some of that." My words sounded surprisingly wistful—and wise.

I gave myself a mental pat on the back.

Maybe I could work that line into one of my movie scenes.

"Of course. Some people thought she'd compromised who she really was. Given in to 'the man.'" Todd's face brightened as if he had a memory. "This one guy thought she stole his song."

My breath caught. "I've done a lot of research, and I've never heard that."

"Emma Jean didn't even like to talk about it."

"Do you remember this guy's name?"

"As a matter of fact, I do. His name was Cyrus Pitts. I remember because I thought he was the pits. He tried to make a go at music around here, playing at some local restaurants. He wasn't that good. That's putting it nicely."

"Where did this Cyrus Pitts guy live?"

"It just so happens he went to school with Emma Jean, and he still lives in town. He claimed she took the lyrics they wrote together and made millions off of them. Meanwhile, he owns a music store in town—no one is sure how it even stays open, but it does."

It sounded like I had my first lead to track down.

I planned on following up . . . right after I met with the cast and crew.

I thanked him and took a step away. But as I walked toward my car, I paused in the lot and glanced around.

Why did I have that eerie feeling that someone was watching me?

I scanned the street in front of me but saw nothing.

So why did I feel this way?

Then I saw him.

A man with pale skin wearing all black. He ducked into the shadows in a patch of woods as soon as I turned toward him.

Had that been Ezra?

A chill washed over me.

Suddenly, I felt like Bella in *Twilight* when Edward Cullen was watching out for her.

The difference here was: I didn't want Ezra watching out for me . . . especially since I had no idea what his intentions were.

As I rushed toward my car, it felt as if a fire had been lit under my feet.

Out here, I felt exposed, and I needed to get somewhere safe . . . and fast.

chapter
ten

I **SPENT** the next three hours blocking scenes.

Selby had rented an old house that looked similar to the one Emma Jean had grown up in. We had it for the next three months since several scenes would be shot there.

The scenes we were working on today took place when Emma Jean was a teenager, right before she was discovered. They mostly involved me sitting on the bed with a guitar, lip syncing and occasionally talking to my mother or to my boyfriend on the phone.

Overall, it was pretty simple.

As I pretended to be Emma Jean, I couldn't help but put myself in the singer's shoes.

When she'd first gotten her record contract, she must have felt on top of the world.

Then success and fame and all that came with it had caused everything to crash down around her.

The sad truth of the matter was that most people I knew who'd achieved everything they wanted in Hollywood admitted that it had come with a cost.

Sometimes it was relationships. Sometimes it was freedom. Sometimes it was self-respect.

But fame could be like a dangerous drug. When it was taken away, people began to suffer from withdrawal. Others, when they saw big amounts of money being flashed before their eyes, did crazy things to obtain it. The people in their lives felt like they wanted a piece of it, like they *deserved* a piece of it, and that also complicated things.

Selby was running through things one more time when my phone buzzed. I looked at the screen and saw it was a text from Ezra. It appeared his phone was operational again.

How convenient.

I frowned when I read the words.

He was having trouble with the water heater again.

Wasn't that just lovely?

Selby gave me a look, and I quickly put my phone back in my pocket. "Sorry. There are some disadvantages to filming in the area where I live."

"I can imagine. But we're paying you for your time, so just pretend like you're back in Hollywood."

His eyes drooped in an annoyed, I'm-getting-tired-of-you expression.

I got the message loud and clear. I was already on his bad side and needed to shape up.

I focused on more of his directions, trying to give him all my attention.

But in the middle of his speech, I heard a car rumble across the gravel driveway outside.

I rested my hands on top of the guitar I held and asked, "Is someone else supposed to be here?"

A knot formed on Selby's brow. "Not that I know of."

He turned toward the door.

The next moment, Kitty came charging up the stairs and across the deck toward us.

Dread filled me.

More trouble was coming our way.

"I told you I don't want you filming this movie!" Kitty stared at everyone.

She'd barged inside before anyone could stop her, and now she had our full attention.

"If you want to stop this then you need to take legal action." Selby let out a sigh and stepped toward Kitty. "But coming here and threatening us isn't the solution."

I was certain that legal action was the last thing Selby wanted. It would put the brakes on this production for sure.

But Selby was a smart man. I'm sure he'd covered all his bases before sinking any money into this movie. It was only wise—and Selby seemed wise.

"You should all be ashamed of yourselves. Exploiting my deceased daughter like this." Her nostrils flared as she scowled at everyone, accusation in her gaze.

I pressed my lips together.

I felt bad for the woman. I really did.

But she wasn't exactly someone who should be lecturing us about exploiting her daughter. Many people thought that was exactly what she'd done.

From the time Emma Jean was old enough to perform, her mother had put her out there to do just that. It wasn't just at school or church either. Kitty had entered Emma Jean into pageants and talent shows and signed her up for every local fair that came on her radar.

She was a mom-ager, or mom manager.

Some people even blamed Kitty for Emma Jean's death.

No, maybe she hadn't physically hurt her daughter, but certainly she'd put a lot of pressure on her.

"I'm going to make sure this movie doesn't film if I have to stop it myself." Kitty placed her hands on her hips and stared at everyone.

"All right." Selby's tone turned no nonsense. "I'm going to have to ask you to leave."

"You're going to have to make me." Kitty raised her chin.

I glanced at Selby and saw the frustration in his gaze, in the wrinkles on his brow.

Then he let out a long breath and grabbed his phone. "Fine. If you want to do it this way, then we'll do it this way."

He began dialing, no doubt calling the police.

Ten minutes later, two cops showed up and escorted Kitty away kicking and screaming.

A surprising rush of shame filled me.

Maybe I *shouldn't* be a part of this movie. What if by doing so I ruined Kitty's life?

I shook my head. I didn't really see how that was possible. All the information in the movie was already public information in either book or article form. People had been obsessed with Emma Jean's death ever since it happened. Dying young and tragically while being famous tended to do that.

My thoughts continued to race. I was facing a moral dilemma, and I needed to figure out what I was going to do.

But the truth was, it was probably too late to do anything.

I had signed the contract for this movie, and production had begun.

But I was feeling more and more uneasy about *Ragdoll* all the time.

SHORTLY AFTER KITTY had been taken away by the cops, Selby gave the cast and crew a two-hour break. He'd had lunch catered, but instead of grabbing a sandwich, there was something else I wanted to do.

I wanted to go to Orbitz and see if I could find some more information on this Cyrus Pitts guy. His shop was only about ten minutes away.

When I walked in the store, I spotted the man right away.

Tweed driving cap, thick glasses, and an overall turtle-ish look. Even though he was in his late twenties, he gave off an old spirit aura that made him seem at least fifty.

"Can I help you? You looking for some good Rolling Stones originals?"

Rolling Stones original albums? I could get on board with that.

Then I quickly remembered my purpose for being here—and it wasn't shopping.

I glanced around. "Cool place."

He leaned against the glass counter in front of him. "I like it. People keep telling me brick-and-mortar stores are dying, but we're managing to hold steady."

How *did* he manage that?

"You're a musician yourself?" I paused and observed him. "You look like the type."

He beamed brighter. "As a matter of fact, I do some shows on the side. Used to do more, but then I settled down."

I glanced at his ring finger. Based on the gold band there, he appeared to be married.

At once, he squinted, and his countenance changed. "Do I know you?"

"I don't think we've met."

"But you look so familiar . . ."

I shrugged. "Maybe I just have one of those faces."

"Maybe." But he still didn't sound convinced. "So are you in here looking for anything in particular?"

"I'm actually playing Emma Jean Gibbons in a new movie about her life."

"Emma Jean?" He seemed to go ramrod straight at the mention of her name.

"I thought I'd ask you a few questions about her."

"What kinds of questions?"

"Someone told me there's someone in this area she used to collaborate with for her songs. Particularly for 'Ragdoll.'"

His gaze darkened and, when he spoke again, his words came out quickly. "You heard about that? Who told you?"

I shrugged, trying to look casual still. "I just like to ask around. Is it true?"

He jammed his finger into his chest. "We wrote that song together, but she got all the credit."

I lowered my voice, trying to sound conspiratorial. "What do you mean you both wrote it? If that was the case, why isn't your name on it?"

He also lowered his voice as he said, "Because she stole it from me, and I have proof."

My curiosity piqued. "What kind of proof?"

"Emma Jean and I would both write our lyrics down in these leather-bound journals."

"I read in an article that she still liked to do that, even when she became famous."

"Oh, yes. And she acted like those journals were worth a million bucks. She hid them, always afraid someone would find them and steal her songs. Ironic, huh?"

"I'd say."

"I thought the two of us were friends. Some of the best times I've ever had was when we used to write together down by the water. We had this spot—coincidentally, it was in front of the house she later bought—that we thought was so inspiring. My aunt owned the place at the time, and the two of us would stay out there for hours working on lyrics."

"That must have been shocking for you—and made you angry—when she didn't include you as her co-author."

"Oh, I was angry all right. Credit should be given where credit is due."

"I guess maybe Emma Jean wasn't as nice as everyone says."

He let out a breath. "She *used* to be nice. But that Brent Mitchell changed her."

Brent Mitchell was her manager and boyfriend. He had a reputation as a player in the music world.

"He was always riding her case, pushing her to be skinnier, prettier," Cyrus continued. "To write more songs. To jump at every opportunity. I think it wore her down after a while, and she didn't even enjoy music anymore. Fame changed her—and not for the best."

"She told you that?"

"No, but I could read between the lines."

Another customer stepped inside, and I knew our conversation was over.

That was disappointing, but maybe at least I was walking away with some new information.

I thanked Cyrus then exited the store.

As I did, I spotted a man standing at the corner of the building smoking.

Smoking? Just like the man outside my house last night?

As if I was living out a scene in a bad movie, the guy motioned me over. "Psst. Hey, you. I heard you're looking for some information."

I felt like a really bad drug deal was about to go down in broad daylight or something.

But despite that, I wanted to know what this guy had to say.

"Can I help you?" I started.

"I heard you asking about Emma Jean." The guy had an almost James Dean sort of look with his wavy hair brushed back from his face, his laid-back actions and speech, and his smoky gaze.

My gaze went to his shirt. Orbitz had been embroidered on his polo.

He worked for Cyrus Pitts.

"Did you know her?" The guy seemed like the musician type, and maybe he was in his mid-thirties.

"Her songs weren't my style. I'm more into rock. You know, the good stuff? But Cyrus couldn't stand Emma Jean. To this day, he makes snide comments about her."

Sounded like someone with a chip on his shoulder. "Is Cyrus a violent type of guy?"

His eyebrows shot together. "Violent? I don't know about that. But he's been obsessed with that stupid song she'd supposedly stolen years ago. He talks about it every chance he gets. But then he'll change his tune and act like he doesn't care. Kind of weird, you know?"

This guy might have just the information I needed. "What else do you know?"

"I know that two days before she died, Emma Jean came into the music store, and the two of them had it out. There was so much anger in that room that I feared someone would get hurt."

"What were they arguing about?"

"That stupid song, if I had to guess. If I were Cyrus, I'd think she did me a favor by not putting my name on drivel like that. But to each his own."

"How did the argument end?"

"Emma Jean left, and she was crying. She looked pretty upset."

I swallowed hard.

Was Cyrus mad enough to kill Emma Jean over that song he claimed she stole?

That was the question.

chapter
twelve

BACK ON SET, we ran through our lines.

Just as before, I tried really hard to pay attention. But at every opportunity, my thoughts drifted back to Emma Jean.

In the middle of rehearsing, my phone buzzed.

I snuck a glance at the screen and saw it was Ezra. Again.

I hadn't responded to his earlier text, and apparently he was getting antsy about it. I probably should have followed up on my lunch break, but I'd been distracted.

I still had a bad feeling about that guy.

"Is everything okay, Mrs. Darling?"

I glanced up at Selby, suddenly feeling like I'd been caught passing notes in science class.

I shoved the phone in my pocket. "Sorry again. I'm

trying to balance some things with Jackson being out of town."

"I'm going to have to ask people to leave their phone in a jail 'cell' when they arrive, just like I do with my kids at dinnertime."

"I'm sorry. I'll keep it in my pocket for the remainder of our time together. I promise."

Selby gave me another look that made it clear I was getting started on the wrong foot with him.

Go figure.

Finally, the workday ended.

As soon as I stepped outside, I ran into Bryant James as he headed toward the house.

He was the last person I wanted to see, but I decided to be polite.

"Hey," I started. "I didn't realize that you were going to be here."

I stared up at him. His oval-shaped face was clean-shaven, and every single one of his light-brown hairs were in place.

He looked like a trustworthy guy. But there was something about him that made me uneasy.

"Selby said I could stop by whenever I wanted so I thought I'd check and see how things are going," Bryant said. "How are things on the set?"

"Just fine." I figured it was best to keep my response simple.

"I'm glad to hear that. I have to say, I thought you were really perfect for this role. I'm glad you said yes." He stared at me, as if trying too hard to read my expression.

"I'm pretty excited about it also." I didn't acknowledge the fact that I'd just been having some doubts earlier.

As Bryant shifted, I knew he had something else on his mind. I waited for him to get to the heart of the matter.

"Listen, I heard about what happened to you this summer." His eyes suddenly looked beady and hungry.

I cocked an eyebrow. "This summer?"

I had a vague idea of what he was talking about, but I certainly wasn't going to make this any easier for him.

"About that woman who was impersonating you."

What had happened wasn't exactly a secret. In fact, for a time, the news was plastered across the headlines.

This past summer, a woman had pretended to be me. In fact, I'd thought she was going to kill me and try to take over my life.

Turned out, she'd only planned to keep me in her basement while she took over my life.

Not ideal, by any means.

Thankfully, that hadn't happened, and the woman was now in prison.

And potentially my half-sister. That was a whole other story, however.

Bryant licked his lips like a snake about to strike before saying, "I also heard that another man might be your father."

The blood drained from my face.

My heart nearly stopped.

Where had Bryant heard that? I *definitely* hadn't made that information public.

I swallowed hard as I fought to maintain my composure. "I don't know what you're talking about."

He stepped closer, a greedy gleam to his eyes. "I think you do."

I raised my chin, uncomfortable with the cockiness in his tone. "What are you getting at?"

"I want to write your story."

"If only there were a story to be written." I tried to brush past him, but he grabbed my arm.

I stared at his hand on my bicep until he released it.

"Look, I'm not trying to be a pain." He shoved hands into pockets as if to not be tempted to grab me again. "But I'm always looking for a good story, and I think you have one."

"My story is *my* story. Whatever you think you know, you don't."

The last thing I needed was for Bryant to go public with some story my dad might end up hearing. If my dad wasn't actually my dad then I needed to be the one to tell him—not some slimy, arrogant journalist.

"It could make you a lot of money, you know." He said the words as if he tried to sound enticing.

"I'm not interested in money. That's not the most important thing in life."

I tried to walk away again when Bryant called to me.

Hesitantly, I paused and turned toward him. "Yes?"

My voice sounded clipped and impatient—just as I intended. I couldn't let this guy walk on me—or intimidate me.

"You should think about it." The enticement disappeared from his voice, replaced by an almost threatening tone. "Because I'd rather get you on record."

A bad feeling filled my gut.

This was what had happened with Kitty, wasn't it?

It was either she talked to Bryant, or he'd write the story his way without her input.

A rock closed in on me on one side and a hard place on the other.

Boy, did I wish that Jackson were here.

I could really use his insight.

But I didn't want to distract him during his training. He needed to be able to concentrate, and I didn't want my problems to always be at the center of his thoughts. He deserved this time to himself.

Before Bryant could ask me any more questions, I hurried away.

However, the bad feeling continued to linger in my gut.

As I left from filming, I called my best friend, Phoebe Waters.

I'd hired her to help me take care of Ripley while I worked. She'd stopped by at lunchtime to take him for a long walk on the beach.

That was what she did. She took care of animals while also working at Oh Buoy.

She was currently dating Sam Butler, one of my costars from *Relentless*. I was thrilled that their relationship had worked out because they both seemed truly happy. And I was happy for them.

She'd agreed we could meet for dinner.

Notice how I had this eating out theme in my life? I wasn't denying it. But going somewhere to eat was so much more fun than actually cooking for myself and having dirty dishes to clean.

We'd decided to meet at The Fatty Shack. The place

had been one of my dad's favorite restaurants. It was located on the causeway between Manteo and Nags Head, and it looked like an old fishing shanty. Even inside, there were crab pots and buoys that served as decorations.

My autographed picture also hung on the wall, along with a smattering of other celebrities who'd eaten there.

I headed to the restaurant, and by the time I arrived, Phoebe was already sitting in a booth.

There were some nice things about the offseason here in the Outer Banks. Being seated quickly was one of them. In the summer, we would have had a two-hour wait to get a table.

But in the winter . . . it was a local's game. I, for one, loved it.

I slid into the booth across from Phoebe and saw she'd already ordered some hushpuppies. Yes, thank you. I'd definitely take some of those if she offered.

"So, what's been going on?" Phoebe grabbed a hushpuppy and pulled it apart, watching the steam escape from the inside.

That question was the only thing I needed.

Phoebe was a great listener. So I poured out everything to her, and she listened, nodding at all the appropriate times. I didn't hold back as I practically did a word vomit at the booth.

When I finished, she raised her eyebrows. "Wow. That sounds like a lot. Like *a lot* a lot."

"I know, right? I think I'm losing my mind." I frowned as I watched her reaction, waiting for her to confirm my fears.

"Okay, so there are a lot of things we should talk about." She nodded slowly as if mentally sorting through what I'd told her. "But for starters, you really think that Emma Jean was murdered?"

"I can't get the thought out of my mind," I admitted.

"Who would have the motive to kill her?" Phoebe grabbed another hushpuppy.

"An excellent question. Any number of people."

Then I began to list them. Her mom—for the money. Cyrus—out of anger. Maybe even a crazy fan. Todd—after all, Emma Jean had looked nervous at the pharmacy with him. What about Brent Mitchell, her agent/manager/boyfriend? Todd hadn't spoken highly of him. However, he didn't live in this area. So if he hadn't come this way for a visit, I'd need to rule him out.

"It looks like you have some investigating to do," Phoebe murmured.

I frowned again. "It looks like I do."

As I said the words, that chill came over me again.

I glanced around, looking for the source of it.

"Joey?" Phoebe stared at me.

Instead of responding, I rose and walked toward the window.

I was just in time to see a man walking away . . . a man wearing a black cape.

Was that . . . Ezra? Was he following me?

My blood—which very well could be very tasty—went cold at the thought.

Just what was that man planning?

I EXPLAINED the situation to Phoebe when I got back to the table.

We talked about it a few minutes before turning the conversation back to Emma Jean.

We were in the middle of eating when someone sauntered up to our table.

I held my breath, halfway expecting to see Ezra.

Instead, my good friend Zane Oakley stood there.

Just as always, his curly hair was naturally high-lighted by the sun—even in the winter. He was tall with broad shoulders and a lean build, always looking like the quintessential surfer.

We'd been neighbors then friends then had almost dated. Now we were back to being just friends. Zane was a great guy—a great guy with some problems. Now he was dating a woman named Sunshine, a fellow surfer and maker of soy candles. The two of them seemed really happy together.

I hadn't seen him in a couple of months.

I stood and gave him a quick hug.

Then he grabbed a chair and pulled it up to the end of the booth.

He wagged his eyebrows as he glanced back and forth between Phoebe and me. "I smell an investigation. What kind of trouble are you ladies up to now?"

Yes, Zane knew me well. But how much should I tell him?

I contemplated my options a moment, then I glanced at the time.

It was almost seven. If I was going to go to Ezra's house to look at that stupid water heater then I'd need to go soon.

"Joey?" Zane stared at me.

The perfect idea hit me. "I'd be more than happy to fill you in on what's going on. But I was wondering if you might do a favor for me."

"What's that?"

I explained the whole renter situation and how I didn't want to go over there alone.

Zane didn't even think twice before nodding. "Of course I'm in. I just ordered, but I'll take my food to go as long as you drive and I can eat in your car."

I nodded. "It's a deal."

Relief filled me. That had worked out well. Because I'd considered asking Phoebe to go over to the house with me, but I wasn't comfortable with that either.

Ezra set me on edge, to say the least, and I didn't want to take any chances.

On the way to the house, I filled Zane in on everything that was going on—from the movie to the rental situation. He scarfed down his crabcake sandwich as I talked.

"I've always thought there was something weird about Emma Jean's death," Zane said before wiping a blob of mayo from his lips with a napkin.

My eyes widened as I looked at him. "You too? I know, right? I mean, why doesn't everyone else see it?"

"There is no way she accidentally died on the way to commit suicide."

I leaned back in my seat, feeling slightly more satisfied to know that my friend was seeing things eye to eye with me.

"Now, enough about me," I murmured. "What's going on with *you*?"

Zane told me about how well things were going with Sunshine, how he loved his new-ish job as a real estate agent, and how he finally felt as if he was straightening out his life.

By the time he finished, we'd pulled up to the rental, and I put the car in Park.

What would I find inside this time? Part of me didn't want to know.

"You actually look kind of nervous." Zane glanced at me before shoving his empty food containers back into the plastic bag they'd come in.

I shrugged. "Maybe I am. I don't know."

"You can never be too careful when you're as well-known as you are," Zane said. "People will do all kinds of crazy things if it means getting close to you. But I'm sure I don't have to tell you that."

No, he didn't have to tell me that. I knew it all too well. My Super Stalker Fan Club came to mind.

But hearing his words out loud sent a shiver through me.

No one should know that I was the owner of this place. It wasn't exactly as if Jackson and I advertised the house as a two for one deal. Rent our house, meet Joey Darling.

No, the place was under Jackson's name, with no hints I was associated with it. I supposed if someone dug deep enough, they would find I'd married Jackson, and they may have put things together.

I pushed those thoughts aside when Zane shifted in his seat.

"Let's just get this over with," Zane said. "Then, in the future, maybe you should consider going with a management company."

Zane *would* say that. He was now working in real estate, and oftentimes in this area real estate and vacation management companies went hand in hand.

When we climbed the front steps, a slight sense of relief filled me when I noticed the door wasn't wide open this time.

I peered inside through the pane of glass in the top of the door.

That table for two remained set with the candles burning, almost all the way down to the holders at this point.

What exactly was going on with this guy?

On second thought, I really didn't want to know.

But I knew it was too late to back out now.

Before I could say anything, Zane knocked at the door.

I waited to see what this guy was going to say or do next.

I **WAS ALMOST** ready to tell Zane we should leave. Several minutes had passed, and Zane had knocked three times—which seemed like ample time.

Before we turned away, the door opened, and Ezra stood there.

His gaze slid from me to Zane then back to me. "You brought someone."

Not *you brought help*. Not *you brought a plumber*.

But *you brought someone*.

The way Ezra had worded his statement sounded odd.

"I figured if you were still having water heater issues then I probably wasn't the one to help you fix it," I finally said. "But Zane here is a jack-of-all-trades."

Ezra stared at Zane again, a cold look in his eyes.

I didn't like Ezra, I decided. At first, I'd thought it was just me and my overblown imagination.

But it was more than that.

This guy gave me the heebie-jeebies.

"Come on in," Ezra said.

Even though this was my home, part of me didn't want to step foot inside.

Part of me didn't want to close that door.

Maybe I'd watched *Twilight* too many times because I halfway expected Ezra to randomly show us his fang-like teeth or for the man to suddenly turn into a bat.

"I guess you know where the water heater is." Ezra's voice sounded dull and maybe even annoyed.

"I do," I quipped. "But let me show Zane."

Zane followed me as I headed down the hallway and turned into the laundry room, which also served as the water heater closet. There were also some shelves along one wall where people could store nonperishable food.

My gaze stopped on a box of Count Chocula.

Vampire-themed cereal. Coincidence? I think not.

Zane stepped inside, and I stayed close, just to be safe. Ezra remained on our heels.

"So what's going on?" Zane paused by the water heater and glanced at Ezra.

"Water's not getting hot." Ezra crossed his arms. "I

wondered if something might be wrong with the water heater. I, for one, do not enjoy a cold shower."

"No, I can understand that." Zane began to inspect the water heater.

I had no idea what he was looking at or why he put his ear close to the heater as if listening for something. But he did.

"Everything looks and sounds okay to me." Zane tapped the metal tank with his knuckle. "Let me go test out the water in the bathroom so I can see for myself what's wrong."

"It heats," Ezra said. "It just takes a long time."

"That's not exactly unusual," Zane said. "The water takes time to travel through the pipes."

I could read between the lines. I didn't think anything was wrong with the water heater. I thought Ezra wanted to get me over here for some reason.

To suck my blood maybe?

As Zane walked into the bathroom, I lingered in the hallway. So did Ezra.

Was that because he didn't want us to know he didn't have a reflection?

I glanced at the dining room table. Before I could speak, I noticed that the cross I'd had hanging on the wall was now gone.

My throat tightened.

Had he taken it down?

I'd really just been being silly with the vampire stuff. But maybe there was some truth to it.

I cleared my throat and nodded toward the table. "It looks like you're expecting someone."

Ezra's gaze darkened. "Something like that."

"Please be careful with the candles. Those are getting a little low, and the wax could get on the table. I intended to put it in the contract that we prefer no candles in the house, just as a precaution."

He stared at me, a strange look in his eyes.

A steely look that made my blood go cold.

Then he stalked to the dining room table and blew the candles out.

Ezra turned back toward me, robotic in his motions. "Happy now?"

He didn't ask it sarcastically. No, he sounded sincere, like he only wanted to please me.

"Thank you." My voice sounded strained. "I hope your date doesn't mind."

"I don't think she will." His gaze lingered on me.

The skin on my neck rose.

Was he trying to get me over here so I could be his date?

I wanted to get out of here.

Now.

Bringing Zane with me was one of the best choices I'd made lately.

"I think the water is going to be just fine." Zane stepped into the hallway. "It's an old hot water heater, so it might take a while to heat up. Plus, it's electric not gas so it always takes longer. You just have to be patient."

Ezra's gaze remained on me as he said, "Thanks."

Zane put his hand on my arm and placed himself between me and Ezra. "We'll let you get back to your evening."

"I'm sorry you're having problems with the house," I murmured.

Ezra shrugged. "No, I'm sorry to call you out here for no good reason."

Instead of seeing us out, he watched us cross the room.

I still expected those fangs to appear or for the man to turn into a bat at any moment.

But that didn't happen.

Zane ushered me outside, we waved goodbye to Ezra, and then we hurried back to my car. If only I'd thought to bring some garlic with me.

"That guy was creepy," Zane said as we started back down the road.

"So it's not just me?"

"No way. There's something totally off about him."

"I think so too."

"You did the right thing by asking me to come with you. I don't even want to think about what that guy might have been planning if you'd come alone."

I shivered, taking one hand off the steering wheel long enough to run it over my arm. I felt goosebumps beneath my jacket.

"What should I do?" I asked as I stared at the dark road ahead.

"How many more days is he renting this place?"

"For the rest of the week."

"When does Jackson get back?" Zane asked.

I'd told Zane earlier that Jackson was doing some training in Raleigh. "His workshop isn't over until Friday, so he'll get home that evening."

Based on Zane's grunt, he didn't like that update.

"What does Jackson say about this?" Zane asked.

The two had been rivals, but I thought Zane had truly come to respect Jackson.

I inwardly cringed. "I haven't exactly told him."

Zane looked at me, a crease between his eyes. "Why not?"

"Because I want to prove that I can handle this myself, that I'm not incompetent." Wasn't that the real reason? I wanted to be good at something besides acting.

"I'm sure he doesn't think you're incompetent."

"Maybe not. But there was that article that came out in a magazine calling me a Pampered Princess."

Zane did a double take at me. "I thought you didn't take those things too seriously?"

"I try not to," I said. "But then I started thinking that maybe there was some truth to what was being said in the article. I don't want to be someone whom people think is waited on hand and foot. I want to be able to stand on my own two feet."

"I think you've already proven that you can. The time since when you got divorced from jerk-face Eric Lauderdale until you got married to Jackson . . . you established your own life. You got back on your feet. You built your career. You turned your back on your old way of living and reinvented yourself."

Zane's words caused me to flush.

Probably because they were so kind.

Also because it meant so much to me that someone had noticed all my hard work. People mostly seemed to notice my flaws.

"Thank you." My voice came out as a squeak.

"I mean it. Don't let anybody tell you that you're not doing a good job, Joey."

"Jackson has never said I wasn't doing a good job."

I felt the need to clarify that. "Maybe I just want to prove it to myself."

"You have nothing to prove to anyone. I think Jackson would agree with me."

I thought he would agree with that also. But it meant a lot to me that Zane was being supportive—of both me and Jackson.

Zane glanced at me. "If this guy contacts you again, don't go to the house alone. Promise me?"

I didn't have to think about it for long. "I won't."

"Thank you."

I hoped that Ezra had gotten the message and wouldn't be texting again.

But why did I seriously doubt that?

BACK AT THE HOUSE, I gave Ripley some good head pats before letting him outside into the dog run. I had some things I wanted to do—including looking into both Maverick and Bobbi.

But first, I called Jackson.

"Hey, gorgeous," he answered.

"Hey. Am I calling at a bad time?" I leaned back in the chair, hot cocoa in hand.

"Never. How was your day?"

I contemplated how much to say. Tell him about Ezra or not?

Since I'd pretty much decided I wasn't going over there again, I decided not to tell him. Knowing Jackson, he'd drop everything and come home. Or he'd stay there and worry. That wasn't what I wanted.

I decided to stay quiet.

Instead, I told him about filming and eating with Phoebe.

"It sounds like you're getting along just fine without me," he said.

"I don't know if I'd say that . . . I miss you bunches."

"Bunches?"

"That's right . . . just like grapes."

Just like grapes?

Man, I really had a way with words. Emma Jean would have said something beautiful, poetic, and that was sure to become an earworm.

"Well, I miss you too. I can't wait to get back home."

Warmth filled me. I couldn't wait for him to get back either. Now that Jackson was a part of my life, I couldn't imagine my future without him. I wanted us to have children and grandchildren and to grow old together.

Just then, Ripley started barking outside, and I knew I needed to wrap up this conversation. "I should go let him in."

"He does get awfully impatient sometimes, doesn't he?"

"Yes, he does." I paused, hating to say goodbye. But Ripley had left me with no choice. "I love you. I can't wait to see you."

"Love you too. Be safe."

If Jackson only knew.

I rose from my comfy seat and walked toward the door.

Except when I reached it, Ripley wasn't there.

He was, however, still barking.

"Ripley!" I called.

He didn't come.

I frowned.

It was cold outside, and the last thing I wanted was to go out there and drag the canine inside. But if I didn't, my neighbors might complain.

Without slipping on my shoes or a coat, I stepped out and climbed down the steps. "Ripley!"

He continued to bark, the sound fast-paced and nearly frantic.

Was there a raccoon or other critter out here?

That seemed like the most logical explanation.

I reached the ground and saw Ripley barking at the fence. Even when I called him, he didn't turn to me.

The hairs on the back of my neck rose.

I glanced at the sidewalk in the distance.

That was when I saw the small orange light.

The light from a cigarette.

Just like I'd seen last night.

This time, the light didn't move.

Almost as if someone stood there watching my house . . . or watching me.

Ripley had sensed the danger, hadn't he?

My throat squeezed until I could hardly breathe.

Who would that be? The guy who'd been outside of Orbitz? Someone who despised me for being part of this biopic? One of Adolf's guys?

Quickly, I grabbed Ripley's collar and pulled him back inside the house. Then I locked the door and called the police. It was the responsible thing to do.

Until they arrived, I'd sit in the corner with Ripley beside me and my phone in my hand, just in case that man tried to get inside.

chapter
sixteen

TWO OFFICERS HAD SHOWN up last night after I put in a call to the police.

Both were friends of Jackson's, of course.

Which meant I'd need to tell my husband what had happened before his colleagues did.

Men in blue looked out for each other like that.

Unfortunately, by the time the cops had arrived, the man with the cigarette was gone.

But I knew I'd seen that man twice now and that his presence wasn't a coincidence. Someone was watching my house.

Could Adolf be watching? Had he sent someone else to watch me?

He *had* been an agent with the CIA, and he'd made lots of enemies, specifically with the Russians. The Russians weren't people you wanted to mess with.

I didn't think that Ezra was out there, and he didn't strike me as a smoker either. I'd seen no evidence of that in the rental.

Nor did I think it was anyone affiliated with the movie. I hadn't done anything to get anyone's suspicions riled up.

Not yet.

The man's presence outside my home made me uneasy.

Currently, I was driving toward the set so I could begin another day of working on *Ragdoll*.

Unfortunately, when I pulled up to the house, I immediately knew that something was wrong.

Eight cars were parked out front along with a couple of vans.

There was nothing strange about that. So what was this feeling for?

I climbed out of my car and slowly walked toward the rickety porch.

Selby met me there. The look in his eyes was stormy, to say the least.

"Joey, I'm glad you're here." He hurried down the steps and took my elbow, directing me away from anyone inside who might be listening.

The tension between my shoulders grew tighter. "What's going on?"

"There's an update I wanted to tell you about. I

wanted you to hear it from me first."

Now he *definitely* had my attention. I glanced up at him and crossed my arms over my chest as I prepared to hear whatever it was he had to say.

"Somebody broke into Kitty's home last night," he started.

I gasped. "What?"

"The police think it was a robbery turned home invasion turned assault with a deadly weapon."

"What happened? Is she okay?"

"It appears there was a struggle. Maybe Kitty was defending herself. She was shot."

I gasped again. "Is she . . . dead?"

"No, she's not. But she's sedated at the hospital right now. They're probably going to transfer her up to the trauma care facility in Norfolk."

"I'm really sorry to hear that."

His lips tightened again. "There's something else."

"Okay . . ." What else could there be?

"We have to pause production right now."

"Because Kitty's in the hospital? You mean like out of respect for that situation?" I tried to process what he was saying.

"No, because the police want to talk to me."

"What?" My voice climbed with surprise.

"I'm sure it's just a formality. But I guess somehow

it got back to them that there was bad blood between Kitty and me."

"The cops think you did this?" I didn't mince my words.

Selby shook his head a little too quickly. "Of course not. They just want to talk to me."

But I was no fool.

Selby was most likely the prime suspect right now. He simply had the strongest motive to hurt Kitty.

The question was, would he have really taken things this far in order to protect his investment?

My schedule had unexpectedly opened up.

Now I needed to figure out what to do with myself.

I knew I should be disappointed we weren't filming. I knew this role could do great things for my career, kind of like Joaquin Phoenix in *Walk the Line* or Jamie Foxx in *Ray*.

The fact was my theory kept floating through my mind and wouldn't leave my thoughts.

Something just didn't seem right about the way Emma Jean died.

I knew I could be reading too much into the situation. But I stood behind my theory. However, I had nothing to prove her death had been malicious.

Based on what I knew so far, if anyone had killed Emma Jean and made it look like an accident, Cyrus Pitts was the most likely suspect—he believed Emma Jean had stolen his song.

Had Kitty discovered that? Confronted him?

Was that why she'd been shot?

That could be a stretch.

I wondered why Cyrus hadn't taken any legal action against Emma Jean. That seemed to be the most natural recourse in situations like that. But somehow he'd found enough money to start that music store, and to keep it open. I felt like there was more to that story.

For that reason, I hopped back in my car and headed to downtown Manteo. I found a parking space on the street and then climbed out. Today was milder than it had been lately, and I only needed a light jacket.

A few minutes later, I stepped inside Orbitz. "Unchained Melody" was playing overhead, and I couldn't help but pause for a moment and test my lip-syncing skills.

I was on point.

As soon as I saw Cyrus behind the counter staring at me, I dropped my arms and softened my expression.

"Impressive," Cyrus murmured before scowling. "You again. What brings you this way?"

I couldn't tell if there was animosity in his voice or not. But I plastered on a smile anyway. "I'm still researching and trying to get into Emma Jean's headspace."

"That's right. You're that celebrity. You're one of those performers who's into method acting, aren't you?" He said the words with disdain.

"I am."

"Does that mean if you play a character who hadn't showered in thirty days that you wouldn't?" A veiled insult crouched beneath his words.

"I don't think I'd take things that far." His question threw me for a loop, though I had heard of other actors who'd done that.

Jared Leto had supposedly sent dead animals to castmates to get into character for *Suicide Squad*. Christian Bale had lost sixty some pounds for *The Machinist*.

"You want to know who else is still in this area who knew her?" He tapped his finger on the glass countertop and stared off into the distance a moment. "I'm assuming you've heard of Maverick Price."

"Emma Jean's high school boyfriend?" I remembered Glenn telling me about him.

"He's the one," Cyrus said. "He should be able to

tell you a lot about Emma Jean. The two of them were tight. Everyone thought they would get married."

"Wasn't that weird that the two of them were so tight, yet you and Emma Jean also hung out a lot and wrote music together?"

He shrugged, a new aura coming over him—a smugness if I had to guess. "Emma Jean was my friend, and we enjoyed being together. Emma Jean always preferred to hang out with guys over gals. Said guys were less catty."

Maybe that explained her friendship with Todd.

"That's more than I can say about her and Maverick," Cyrus continued. "I never understood what kind of connection she could have with the high school quarterback. They were nothing alike."

Did I detect an edge of jealousy in his voice?

Maybe.

That added even more motive to this.

I leaned closer, trying to be casual. "So, after Emma Jean hit it big time, when was the last time you saw her? Did she come around a lot? Did she ever want to hang out anymore?"

Cyrus rolled his eyes. "No, she seemed too big for her britches. She came strutting into town like she owned the place. She forgot her roots, and everybody around here knew that. They might not say it in an interview or in front of out-of-towners. Saving face is kind of important, you know. And we all *were* very proud of her. But we weren't beneath her. We were the ones that raised her up."

Interesting. I stored that away in the back of my mind.

"So after she left, that was pretty much it for your friendship, right?"

His gaze clouded. "That's right."

"You said Maverick is still around here?"

"He is. He runs a parasailing outfitter down at the harbor. They even run in the winter, apparently. They bundle people up and take them up in the skies."

I knew exactly where I was headed next.

chapter
seventeen

I **FOUND** the office for Maverick's parasailing business. He'd just left on the boat with four people. Parasailing in the winter? I'd never heard of such. But I supposed with a wetsuit, it could work. After all, people kiteboarded and surfed in the winter . . .

The woman behind the desk told me the group should be back in forty minutes.

I decided to wait. Why not? There was nothing else I could do, and he'd be back within the hour.

So I sat back on a wooden bench overlooking a small harbor, where the parasailers had left from.

My thoughts continued to turn over.

I still wanted to track down Bobbi Sawyer, Emma Jean's best friend from high school. But I'd Googled her and hadn't found anything. Glenn had said she taught private music lessons, but I couldn't find any references to those either. That would make her a challenge to find, but I felt certain that talking to her could be valuable.

Cyrus definitely sounded as if he had a reason not to like Emma Jean. He was holding a grudge. But was that reason enough to kill her? And why had he never taken legal action against her?

The thing that kept coming back to me was that maybe he'd been paid off. It was the only thing that made sense.

Then there was this Maverick guy I was waiting to talk to, the one who supposedly didn't have anything in common with Emma Jean even though they'd dated.

Yet she had dumped him when she left for Nashville. How had he taken that heartbreak?

But again, would that motivate him enough to kill her?

Before I could think about it too long, my phone buzzed.

I glanced at the screen and saw that the alarm at the rental house had been triggered.

My stomach sank.

Not Ezra again.

I needed to check this out. But I remembered promising Zane that I wouldn't go there alone.

I needed to figure out how to handle this.

Renting out this old house was suddenly seeming like a terrible idea.

After staring at my phone for several minutes, I did the wisest thing I could think of.

I called the alarm company.

They gave me a code to punch in to turn off the alarm.

I thanked them and then called Ezra.

He didn't answer.

Which meant the alarm was still going off.

Wasn't that great?

I wouldn't go over there alone just in case this was some type of ruse on Ezra's part to turn me into the undead.

I knew Dizzy had a full schedule at the hair salon today. She'd told me that earlier.

I also knew that Phoebe was working at Oh Buoy until just after lunchtime, at which point she would walk Ripley for me.

I could call Zane, but I wanted to be careful not to get too cozy with him while Jackson was out of town.

That left . . . well, no one.

I frowned.

If I left now, I could probably still be back here in

time to meet Maverick. The house was about a fifteen-minute drive. I just needed to hustle.

I started driving that way, unsure exactly what my plan of action was—which was never a good sign.

But when I pulled into the driveway, I spotted a police car parked out front.

That was right. When the alarm had gone off, the security company automatically sent a message to law enforcement.

Jackson had made sure that was the case.

Relief washed through me.

I pulled in behind the squad car and climbed out, feeling better now that I knew someone else was here.

Before that, I'd figured I would drive past and check out the situation as I tried to figure things out.

When I saw Officer Danny "Loose Lips" Jones on the deck, I suddenly felt much better.

There was no one else I liked to talk to more.

I'd kind of gotten him in trouble once when I tricked him into telling me some information he wasn't supposed to share. He'd left the department for a while. But not before he'd gotten drunk and spontaneously married a Russian spy who'd stolen information from him.

But it had all worked out in the end. He'd been a security guard for the summer, but now he was back on the force on a probationary period.

He spotted me and came down to meet me. "Got a notification about the alarm."

"Is everything okay?" I asked as I paused at the bottom of the stairs.

"Seems to be. No one is home. Or no one's answering, at least."

"I have a code I can use to turn it off," I told him. "Would you mind walking in with me?"

"Not at all."

We headed up the steps together. I used the keypad code on the door to unlock the house. Once inside, I reached for the alarm control pad and punched in the code.

The shrill, high-pitched noise ceased.

Perfect.

Before closing the door, I glanced back at the dining room table.

This time there was no longer a place setting for a romantic dinner for two.

That made me feel a little better.

But I still didn't trust this Ezra guy.

I closed the door and locked it before walking back down the steps with Officer Loose Lips.

"How's Jackson doing at the training?" he asked.

"He seems to be having a good time."

"Glad to hear that. I'm hoping to go myself sometime." He sounded wistful as he said the words.

We paused by his car, and I studied him a moment. "How are you doing, Danny?"

He thought about it a few seconds before shrugging and nodding. "Just fine. Thanks for asking."

"Of course." I shifted, not in a hurry to leave.

Part of me did feel a little guilty. Because I wanted to know what Danny knew about Kitty. But I didn't want him to think I was being friendly just to find out information. *And* I didn't want to get him in trouble again. I really did think he was a nice guy.

I wanted to be careful how I proceeded.

"So I heard about Kitty Gibbons."

He let out a long, slow breath and shook his head. "Isn't that crazy?"

"Absolutely. Who would have done something like that?"

"Apparently, there's a long list of suspects. That's not even including the people working on that movie." He seemed to realize what he said and clamped his mouth shut. "But I guess you already know that."

"You really think someone working on the movie would have done this?"

"Maybe. I heard Kitty Gibbons was as mad as a hornet that this movie was being made. She vowed to do everything in her power to shut down production. The fact you guys were filming here in Manteo? That was just the icing on the cake. She felt as if you guys were invading her turf."

Okay, so Loose Lips actually knew a lot more than I'd guessed—and he'd shared it with me.

I was thankful, plus a little worried about him.

"I'm surprised she didn't have a better reputation in town with her daughter being Emma Jean and all," I said.

"Kitty had a long history with drug use, and she's started a lot of trouble with a lot of people. She's the kind that, as they say, can't keep her mouth shut. If she doesn't like someone, she's going to tell them. That's caused some hard feelings."

I could see that. "I bet. I hope she's okay."

"We all do," Danny said. "She's had a hard life."

"I know she has. I can't even imagine what she went through when she lost her daughter."

"I was friends with some people who knew their family. Not close or anything. But I heard she went into a deep depression, and she hasn't been the same since then."

My heart pounded with compassion. I was sorry to hear that. It showed me a different side of her, one entirely more likable and relatable.

Bryant had painted her as someone just out for money, who wanted to exploit her daughter for every penny she could get. But life was rarely that black-and-white. Emotions came and went like the tide. They overlapped like saltwater and freshwater merging where the ocean and rivers met.

I thanked Officer Danny before climbing back into my car.

I still wanted to see if I could catch Maverick before he left again for another parasailing adventure.

If I timed it just right, I might catch him.

I took one last glance at the house before putting my car into Reverse.

I squinted.

Had the curtain in the upstairs bedroom just moved?

I wanted to believe I was seeing things. But I really didn't think that I was.

Ezra was inside the house this whole time, wasn't he?

There was definitely something going on with that man.

I had no idea where he'd left his vehicle when he set up this stunt.

I also had no idea what kind of game he was playing.

But in this case, I wasn't sure I wanted to find out.

I GOT BACK to the parasailing office just in time.

The boat was back, and several people wandered the docks, talking about how fun it was.

As they did that, I stepped inside the office/gift shop and glanced around.

I didn't see anyone matching Maverick's description. Yes, I'd looked up a picture of him.

But the woman behind the desk—different from the woman I'd met earlier—was standing there. "Can I help you? Are you looking to parasail?"

Being strung up in the air two hundred fifty feet above the water? In this cold weather? No thank you. Especially not with my luck.

"I'm actually looking for Maverick Price. Do you know if he's around?"

The woman smiled sweetly. "You just missed him.

He left to take a quick lunch break before his next outing."

Disappointment lit inside me. "That's too bad. Thank you."

"Can I help you with something?" The woman sounded sincere.

I turned back toward her. "Do you know Maverick well?"

The woman let out a laugh. "I'd hope so. I'm his mother."

Now she had my total attention.

"Is that right?" I shifted. I needed to think of the best way to frame this. "I understand Maverick and Emma Jean Gibbons were quite the item back in high school. I'm a huge Emma Jean fan."

"I've never seen a happier couple." The woman practically beamed as she said the words. "And a beautiful couple also. I really thought the two of them would get married."

"They were that happy together, huh?"

"They really were." Her smile dimmed. "But then Emma Jean got that record contract, and everything changed."

"Did she break up with Maverick or did he break up with her?"

"They said it was mutual, but I really think Emma

Jean made that decision. Long-distance relationships are hard, you know?"

"I do." I absently glanced at some seashell necklaces hanging by the counter, trying not to look too intense. "I bet you were hoping they might get back together one day."

She shrugged. "I did think about it. I wondered if one day the two of them might get back together again."

"Is your son married now?"

"Oh no. Not yet." The woman leaned closer. "Part of me thinks he's never gotten over her."

"Gotten over who?" a voice said behind us.

I twirled around and saw Maverick standing there.

Maverick, who still looked handsome in a high school quarterback kind of way—just a little older. He was broad with a square face, blondish hair, and an intimidating posture.

He didn't sound happy right now.

"I was just talking to this nice lady," his mom said.

He scowled. "That nice lady is Joey Darling, the actor playing Emma Jean in that new movie."

"What?" His mom placed a hand over her heart. "I had no idea."

"What are you doing here?" He stalked toward me.

"I'm just trying to find out more about Emma Jean, and I wanted to talk to you—"

Nostrils flaring, he pointed at the door. "Get out."

I took a step back. "I didn't mean any harm."

"I don't care. Get out. I never want to see you in here again. Do you understand?"

My heart pounded in my chest as I nodded. "Understood."

"And I hope that stupid movie fails miserably!"

With Maverick still glaring at me, I backed toward the door, almost not wanting to turn my back on the man.

He had come unhinged so quickly.

Was that because he was protective of Emma Jean?

Or because he was harboring a secret?

As I walked back to my car, someone called my name.

I glanced around but saw no one. Only the street, some cars, and some birds flying overhead. Where had that voice come from?

"Over here!"

I glanced up and saw Maggie O'Peters on the balcony of a sprawling white inn located on the water.

"I need to talk to you!" she called.

I raised my eyebrows. Funny. She'd acted as if she wanted nothing to do with me while we were on set.

But I wasn't about to pass this opportunity up

either. If she was flagging me down, it was probably for a reason.

"I'll be right there," I called.

She nodded and hurried back inside.

I had to wander around the building trying to find the front door. But when I walked inside, I noticed the place was exquisite, down to the last detail. The woodwork was intricate and shiny with polish, the decorations were purposeful, and the employees even wore neat uniforms.

As I started toward the steps, Maggie met me.

Fifty-something Maggie was playing Kitty. Wearing the blonde wig, she did an excellent job. She even had her accent and way of speaking down to a science.

The woman was brilliant, and she only picked roles that won her awards.

If things worked out the way Maggie planned, she'd probably win an Academy Award for *Ragdoll* too.

She took my arm and led me outside to a deck facing the water. Unlike the lobby, it was empty out here.

"Are you okay?" I knew she had a good reason for calling me over—especially with everything else going on . . .

She frowned and flicked her hand in the air. "I'm

fine. But I'm worried about what's going on with the film."

"You mean because of Kitty?" I clarified.

"Yes, because of Kitty. Aren't you shaken?"

"The police are saying it was a home invasion gone wrong." I said the words to test the water and get her reaction.

She let out a scoffing laugh. "We both know that's probably not true. Especially with how angry she's been about this movie."

"What do you think happened?" I studied her face, curious about what she'd say.

"I have no idea. I just know that I've been hearing things around this bed-and-breakfast."

Now she really had my attention. "What kind of things?"

"Selby and Kitty were arguing last night about something. I don't know what, but I know it sounded heated."

"That *is* interesting, but you know filming a movie can always be high stress."

"There's more to it than that." Maggie glanced around as if to make sure there was nobody else listening. "Last night, I was outside taking a smoke—"

A smoke? What if the person outside my house hadn't been a man but a woman? Could it have been Maggie?

I stored that possibility aside, though I had no idea why it would be her. She had absolutely no motive—that I knew about.

"I saw Bryant. He got back to the inn late. Really late. I peered out my door to watch him, and I thought for sure he had blood on his clothing."

"What?" My mouth gaped.

She nodded. "That's what it looked like to me. The thing is, I don't think he's had time to wash them or get rid of them, which makes me wonder . . . what if they're still in his room?"

chapter
nineteen

BRYANT SEEMED LIKE A SMART GUY. So if he'd done something wrong, certainly he wouldn't have kept bloody clothing or a murder weapon in his room, right?

Yet that was all I could think about.

What if he *had*?

I needed to get into his room somehow.

Before Maggie went back inside, I called to her one more time. "Is Bryant here?"

"No, he left about thirty minutes ago."

"Do you know what his room number is, by chance?"

She did her famous eyebrow quirk. Seriously, she could do it better than anyone I knew. "He's right across the hall from me. Room 202. Why?"

"Just curious." It was better if she didn't know anything more than that.

I watched as she disappeared inside. But my mind continued to race.

Until it stopped at an idea. A great idea if I did say so myself.

I crept up to the second floor and noted that Bryant's room was located next to an alcove with a vending machine.

I tucked myself into the little nook.

Using my phone, I found the number I was looking for. Then I called room service at the inn and ordered some chocolate chip cookies and two bottles of water.

The woman on the other end promised to be up in five minutes.

I told her to leave the food on the table and that I'd return in a moment.

She agreed.

Then I waited.

I knew this was risky, but it was a chance I had to take.

Finally, I heard someone walking down the hallway. I peered out and saw an employee with a tray in her hand.

Patiently, I waited until she went inside Bryant's room. I listened to the door close. I imagined her leaving the food just as I'd requested on the table inside.

Then I waited for her to leave.

If I wanted this to work, I had to be precise. I'd learned that when I'd pulled a stunt like this as Raven Remington on *Relentless*. I got all kinds of great ideas from those episodes.

However, precision wasn't exactly something I was known for. No, I was entirely too clumsy. The harder I tried for perfection, the further I missed the mark it seemed.

Then I heard it. The door clicked open.

That was my sign.

I had to act.

I waited another breath.

I couldn't be a second too fast or a second too slow.

I peered out just as the server slipped out and walked the opposite way.

Before Bryant's door latched, I darted out and grabbed it, and slipped inside his room without making a sound.

Once inside with the lock turned, I leaned against the door, trying to gain control of my racing heart.

But I didn't have much time to do that.

I needed to move before Bryant came back.

As I glanced around Bryant's room, I scrunched my nose.

The man was a slob. Clothes were everywhere. Breakfast remnants had been left on the top of a dresser. Papers were scattered across his desk, while others had fallen on the floor.

But I didn't have time to ponder his neatness—or lack thereof—now. I needed to get busy.

I started by searching through the clothes scattered about the room. I looked for anything suspicious that might point to the fact Bryant had gone to Kitty's last night.

But every piece of clothing I picked up looked normal. Slightly dirty and smelly, but nothing bloody or that pointed to a crime.

I glanced around the room again, wondering what I was missing. That was when I saw another pile of clothing halfway under the bed.

Ah-ha!

I knelt beside them and began to lift each piece.

But there was nothing on them either.

I rocked back on my heels and frowned. Well, this excursion hadn't gotten me anywhere. All this stealthy sneaking around had apparently been for nothing.

I stuffed the clothes back under the bed, trying to leave everything as I'd found it.

I studied the room one more time, making sure I hadn't overlooked anything.

It didn't appear I had. I wasn't sure what had happened to that supposedly bloody clothing. I suppose Bryant could have taken it with him when he left.

But as I walked past his desk, I paused. The man had set up a printer there.

It appeared he liked to see a hardcopy of what he'd written, maybe to edit it.

I skimmed one of the papers on the top of his desk.

The air left my lungs when I saw some of the words.

Tragically Relentless: The Joey Darling Story.

My mouth dropped open.

Even though I knew I probably shouldn't because I'd only get more upset, I turned the page.

This guy . . . he was writing a biography about me!

After that whole stupid conversation we'd had earlier, he hadn't once let on he was *already* writing my life story.

Anger surged inside me.

I couldn't stop myself from reading more.

From small-town hick to one of the most popular actresses of this decade, Joey Darling hasn't always had an easy life. Some say she did it to herself, from making poor decisions to having bad taste in men. Either way, this Pampered Princess is someone practically begging for attention.

Jerk . . .

As much as I might want to take this whole manuscript with me so I could read it more carefully, I knew I didn't have time for that.

But I wasn't going to let Bryant get away with this.

I quickly flipped through the rest of the pages and saw he only had about fifty pages written so far.

From what I could tell, the book detailed my life growing up in the Virginia mountains. How my mom had left when I was young. How I'd done a couple of school productions before getting a certification as a hairdresser. About how I was discovered by Hollywood.

I paused on the last page.

It looked like Bryant had skipped ahead in time because I didn't see anything about my rise to fame or everything that happened with Eric.

Instead, I read the words. *Then she discovered that her father wasn't really her father, but a man named Adolf Casperson was instead.*

My blood went cold.

Was Bryant making that assumption? Or did he

somehow know for certain that Adolf really was my dad?

My heart thumped into my ears, and I could hardly breathe as I tried to process all my thoughts.

But before I could stand there too long, a rattle sounded at the door.

Someone was coming in, I realized.

And I was about to be caught red-handed.

chapter
twenty

QUICKLY, I ducked into the closet.

I dipped into the shadows and slid the door closed just enough to conceal myself.

Then I heard the room door open.

Part of the room, however, was still visible through the crack I'd left.

Bryant was back.

He paused near his bed and ran his hands through his hair, almost as if he were frustrated or upset about something.

He glanced around and frowned.

I froze.

Did he know someone was in his room? Had I left anything that might be evidence of my presence?

That was when I spotted the cookies and bottled water.

How could I have forgotten to hide them?

My heart beat harder.

If he noticed them, he didn't give any indication of it. Not right now. Instead, he nearly collapsed on the side of his bed and ran his hands over his face.

He was the image of a man in distress.

Why? What was going on that he hadn't let on about?

And perhaps the even bigger question: how was I going to get out of here without being caught? What if he was in his room for the rest of the day? Would I be stuck here?

That wouldn't be good because knowing my tribe, one of them would end up calling the police to report I was missing.

Which was great. It really was. I needed to have people looking out for me. We all did.

But this situation felt a bit sticky right now.

Speaking of calling . . . I carefully pulled my phone from my pocket, put it on silent, and then placed it back. The last thing I needed was a phone call right now to give away my presence.

As Bryant rose, I shrank back again. I prayed he didn't come to the closet and open the door only to find me.

Because even though I didn't think he was a killer,

what if he was? He'd have the perfect opportunity to silence me.

All he had to do was take a pillow and press it over my face . . . it would be a silent death.

I had filmed one too many episodes of *Relentless*. It was the only way I could explain how I could so easily think of the perfect way to murder somebody.

But instead of going to the closet, he went to his desk.

I watched as he began rifling through that manuscript—the manuscript about *me*.

I hadn't put the pages back as I'd found them, I realized. I'd been flipping through them and, when I heard someone at the door, I'd quickly thrown the pages on top of each other. But they weren't neat and tidy.

The cookies and water were also right in front of him.

Bryant, however, didn't seem to notice those things at all. Instead, he stared at that manuscript and frowned.

Was that because he was writing an unauthorized biography of me? Had he had a crisis of conscience?

I kind of doubted it.

What if he already had a publisher for this? What if this book was already in the works, and I was powerless to stop it from being released?

For a moment, I related to Kitty. I related to her being so angry about this biopic.

In fact, if someone tried to do a biopic of my life like this, I'd be livid too.

Bryant muttered something underneath his breath before taking out his phone and texting someone. The speed at which his fingers moved made him look frantic.

What exactly was going on? I had no idea.

But I stayed where I was.

I couldn't let him find me.

I needed to think quickly and figure out what I could do to get out of this.

As the minutes continued to tick by, I watched Bryant.

He wasn't nearly as confident in private as he was in public.

Cockiness tended to be that way. It was usually a cover for horrible insecurity.

But the guy was driving me crazy. He would sit on his bed. Run his hands through his hair. Stand up again. Check his phone again. Sometimes type a message. Look at that manuscript again. Then do it all over.

Was he going to do this all evening?

Then it happened.

He saw the cookies and waters on the corner of his desk.

He picked up a cookie and glanced around.

I wanted to sink into the wall and disappear.

But I couldn't.

Did he have any idea I was here?

I waited, hardly able to breathe.

Then he started toward me.

I closed my eyes and tried to think up an excuse.

But there were none.

Unless I wanted to tell him I was a really big fan, and I wanted his autograph or something. But would he really buy that?

I doubted it. I wasn't even sure I could sell it!

He came closer. Closer.

Then his phone dinged.

He looked at the screen. Veered away. Went to his room door, yanked it open, and stormed outside.

I waited several moments, trying to make sure he didn't come back inside.

Then I knew I had to act.

If I was going to get out of here, it needed to be now. I might not have another chance.

chapter
twenty-one

FIVE MINUTES LATER, I was safely on the sidewalk outside the inn, the very location I'd stood after talking to Maverick.

I hadn't seen anyone as I left, but that didn't mean I was in the clear yet.

I was curious about where Bryant had gone. If I had to guess, he'd jumped in his car and driven somewhere.

If I'd been a little quicker, maybe I could have followed him.

That hadn't gone nearly as smoothly as it did in the movies.

But right now, I was thankful I'd been able to get out in one piece.

I breathed in a deep breath and glanced around.

I was hungry. It was well past lunchtime, and I

hadn't eaten. I needed to find somewhere to grab something fairly quick.

I glanced around the quaint town, and my gaze stopped on a little sandwich shop down the street.

Perfect.

I started walking that way when I saw a woman leaning against an iron fence and staring at me.

Was it because I was a celebrity? I got that quite a bit.

I cast her a quick smile, waiting for her to strike up conversation first. Nothing worse than offering someone an autograph only to realize they were really staring at you because you had toilet paper stuck to your shoe. Been there, done that.

"I hear you've been looking for me," the woman said.

I slowed my steps, not liking the ominous tone to her words. "I have?"

I observed her a moment. Probably in her late twenties. Sleek dark hair, a slender build, and an almost Goth look about her with her black nails, dark clothing, and black choker necklace.

She straightened and nodded. "I'm Bobbi."

Realization spread over me.

Bobbi Sawyer.

Emma Jean's best friend in high school.

I paused in front of her. "I have been looking for you."

"I know." Her gaze remained cool. "What do you want to know?"

She was direct and to the point, and I supposed I couldn't fault her for that. "I was hoping to ask you some questions about Emma Jean. What do you say?"

"That depends. Are you going to use my answers against her?"

"I have no desire to paint her in a bad light," I said. "I want to be accurate with how she's portrayed in the movie."

"Then you won't be basing her story on a book by that bozo Bryant James."

She definitely didn't hold back, and I could appreciate that. "I'm beginning to see that. There are some things in the script that just don't make sense to me, and I'm trying to get some clarity."

"Will that change anything?"

I shrugged, knowing I needed to be honest. "I'm not sure. But I think it's worth a shot."

She stared at me another moment as if trying to surmise whether or not I was trustworthy.

Finally, she nodded. "I believe you. If you treat me to lunch, I'll talk until I'm done eating."

That sounded like a deal to me.

We were seated in a dark, pub-style sandwich shop. The waiter delivered our food surprisingly fast.

I wasn't complaining because I was hungry. My tuna salad sandwich may not have boded well for my breath, but it tasted delightful.

"So what do you want to know?" Bobbi started as she picked up her Italian grinder.

I lowered my sandwich. "I know this is going to sound weird, but there are just some things about Emma Jean's life that don't make sense to me. I can't help but think that maybe her death isn't what everybody thinks it is."

Bobbi's eyes lit up. "That's what I've always thought."

"It is?" I stared at her, grateful to find someone else who agreed with me.

"It just didn't feel right. I mean, Emma Jean and I had drifted apart. I know she'd changed. But I never believed it when the police said how she died."

"What do you think happened?" I picked off a piece of my toasted bread and began to nibble on it.

"I think someone killed her and made it look like an accident. I think they've gotten away with it for five years."

My heart beat harder. "That's what I think too.

But I'm trying to piece together who might have done that to her. Did you have any guesses?"

Bobbi let out a long breath. "It's really hard to say. For a long time, I wondered if maybe it was Cyrus. He was so mad about that song, and I can't say I blame him. I heard the two of them worked on those lyrics for a long time."

"Why would Emma Jean do that to him?"

"I have no idea. It seems pretty underhanded."

"What about Maverick? What are your thoughts on him?"

"He was jealous of the time Emma Jean spent with Cyrus, which was silly because Emma Jean was never interested in Cyrus like that. She was head over heels for Maverick."

"Was Maverick the angry, fly-off-the-handle jealous type or the brooding jealous type?" I remembered the temper he'd displayed when I'd been in his shop earlier.

"He's all testosterone. He was much more reactive back in high school than he is now. I don't think he'd kill Emma Jean. I think he really loved her."

I'd seen some pretty harsh things done in the name of love. But I kept that thought to myself.

"Before she died . . . she had moved back here. Did you keep in touch with her?"

She shrugged coolly, but her frown gave away her true feelings. "She pretty much secluded herself and didn't want to be around people. Maybe she felt ashamed because she'd risen to stardom only to begin to disappear into obscurity again. I know she felt a lot of pressure to stay in the limelight, to remain popular and relevant. I can imagine that's hard."

"It is." I'd been there before.

"However, she did reach out to me, and we had coffee together a couple of times before she passed. I think she was trying to make changes. The last time I spoke with her was about a week before she died. She was really hopeful her new album would do great things for her career."

"Did she say anything strange? I know she was hanging out with Todd from Rusty's Auto Service."

"He was one of the new friends she'd made when she moved back." Bobbi lowered her voice and leaned closer. "Truthfully, I always wondered if her mom was the guilty one."

My eyes widened. I hadn't expected that one. "Why would you think her mom would hurt her?"

"Her mom has always been off-kilter. I know at some point Kitty took out a life insurance policy on her. Since Emma Jean wasn't giving her mom much of the profits from the music, her mom was livid. Said that Emma Jean owed her. Said her daughter would be nowhere without her. Maybe that's true, but Kitty made Emma Jean's life miserable."

"How so?"

"She was always pushing her. Nothing Emma Jean ever did was good enough. She needed more popularity, more money, more fame."

"Why is that?"

"Because Kitty wanted a piece of it." Bobbi shook her head. "Emma Jean had a lot of resentment toward her mom and was ready to write her out of her life."

Kitty probably hadn't handled that well.

My thoughts continued to churn. "Do you know when this life insurance policy was taken out?"

"I'm not sure. I only know that Emma Jean found out about it when she moved back, and she wasn't happy."

"What was it worth?"

"I heard it was two million."

Two million? Was that enough money for a mother to kill her child?

I'd like to think the answer was no.

But I knew that wasn't true.

However, the thought was sobering.

twenty-two

ONE THING BUGGED me as I left the sandwich shop.

If Kitty truly had gotten two million dollars from her daughter's death, then why was she still living as if she were poor?

I hadn't seen Kitty's house for myself. But that was what I had heard.

Now I wanted to see it with my own eyes.

It only took a few minutes for me to find her address online. Then I plugged it into my GPS and started down the road.

Five minutes later, I slowed to a crawl in front of a small cottage resembling the one where filming had been taking place.

It looked remarkably similar. Probably built by the same builder seventy or eighty years ago.

Some improvements had been made to it. The siding appeared to be new and maybe even the windows and roof. But the yard was still in disarray, and the place didn't appear to be well taken care of.

Two million definitely hadn't been poured into it.

Which was strange.

That also made me wonder who got money from the royalties on the songs that Emma Jean had written. They had to be bringing in a decent amount of money.

When I lived in Hollywood, I'd met a guy whose dad had written a hit song back in the eighties. His father had died, and the guy I'd met had begun receiving the royalties from that song. The money was enough that he didn't really have to work another day in his life. He wasn't rich necessarily, but he had enough to survive on.

I had so many more questions now than I had earlier.

Before I drove off, I glanced at my phone. I still hadn't had any updates from Selby. I'd truly expected him to be in touch with me about coming back together to film. After all, he'd reserved the camera crew, and time was money.

But there was nothing.

Which I found suspicious.

I had a lot to think about, and I needed to figure out what I was going to do next.

I decided to head back home for a bit.

On the way, I dialed Selby's number. The best way to find out answers was to ask.

But Selby didn't answer.

I pulled up to my house a few minutes later, went inside, and rubbed Ripley's head.

Then I texted Jackson and asked him if he could call me. I knew there was a good chance he was in the middle of training and couldn't. But I did need to tell him about the alarm thing at the house before Officer Loose Lips had a chance to talk to him.

After I sent the first text, I quickly added that it wasn't an emergency.

But to my delight, my phone rang a moment later.

It was Jackson.

"Hey, sweetheart," he started. "You caught me at a good time."

"I'm glad to hear that. Everything going well?" I sank into the soft couch cushions.

"It's been great." He talked a few minutes about how exciting it was to go through the training program.

"That's great," I murmured.

"How about you? What's going on since I left?"

I hesitated only a minute before telling him about

the alarm going off at the house and Officer Danny coming to help check it out for me.

"I wonder why that went off?" Jackson mumbled.

"I'm not sure." I tucked my legs beneath me. "But our renter this week is a little strange."

"What do you mean by strange?"

"I just mean he's peculiar. He's texted several times about the water heater even though there doesn't appear to be anything wrong with it. And . . . I don't know. He's just different." I felt much better getting that out and not keeping it a secret anymore.

"Maybe he has a crush on you."

"Maybe." Although a crush made it sound a little too innocent.

"Look, if he contacts you again about anything, just call Don. He's a handyman, and I'll have him take care of it. We'll pay him back. I don't want you to have to stress out about this."

Warmth filled me. I loved how Jackson was always looking out for me. "That sounds good."

I mean, maybe I hadn't told Jackson everything. He didn't know how much this guy had given me the creeps or about the weird romantic dinner that had been set up three different times when I had stopped by.

But he knew the gist of it, and that was the important thing.

"Anything else?" Jackson asked. "I have about five minutes until my class starts."

"There is one thing," I started, nibbling on my lip.

I glanced at Ripley, silently asking him if I should ask this or not.

When the canine started panting, I decided that was a sign I should.

I licked my lips before saying, "Kitty Gibbons is in critical care in the hospital."

"I know. I heard about that. Crazy, isn't it?"

"You heard?" That seemed like something he might have called me about if he'd heard.

"I get briefings from the department every morning. But I didn't think much of it. Why?"

"There's speculation that someone associated with the movie is responsible." I was fishing a little bit with that comment, but I felt fairly confident my statement was true.

"Is that right?"

"Now I keep trying to call Selby, and he's not answering his phone. I know for a fact he was brought in to be questioned."

"So you want me to find out more information for you?"

I grinned. Jackson could read my mind.

"Maybe," I said carefully, not wanting to be too pushy.

Jackson didn't say anything for a couple of seconds until finally, "I'll see if I can find out anything, and I'll call you tonight. Okay?"

Hope soared inside me. "That sounds great. Thank you."

"I love you, and I'll talk to you later today."

I ended my call and shoved my phone back into my pocket.

Then I turned back to Ripley. "That wasn't that bad, now was it?"

The dog panted harder, and I rubbed his head.

Then I stood. There was one other thing I needed to do.

I didn't want to do it.

But I had no choice.

twenty-three

I **WALKED** into my office where I'd placed that letter with the DNA results.

What were the chances that Bryant had broken in and stolen my test results?

No, he wouldn't have done that. He'd just been speculating and making it sound as if it were fact. Right?

Despite my reasoning, I continued to stare at the drawer.

Because if what he'd written was somehow true, that meant that my dad wasn't actually my dad, and Adolf was. I still wasn't sure I was ready to accept that.

Though I knew in reality it wouldn't change anything—my dad would always be my dad—I was afraid about how my dad might handle that news. If he would hear it and be devastated. I didn't want to put him through that.

Quite frankly, I didn't want Adolf to be my dad.

It was bad enough that my mom was my mom.

The thought was harsh but true. My mom had left me when I was young and, even though she said it was for my own good, I didn't believe her. She'd chosen her work over me. Maybe in some way it was noble. Maybe if she was working for the CIA then she had done things for mankind I'd never know about. Maybe she'd stopped wars or imminent attacks. Admirable things.

But for an eight-year-old girl without her mom, none of that mattered.

Thankfully, my dad had been a wonderful dad who'd provided much of what I wanted, and everything I needed. He offered me support and unconditional love. And I'd had a great community around me to fill in the blanks.

I still had a lot to be thankful for, and for that I was eternally grateful.

So much of my life had changed. The steadiness of my father had always been constant. And I didn't want to disrupt that.

But I just needed to rip this Band-Aid off.

I stared at the drawer another moment before jerking it open.

The envelope was there. Still staring at me from

beneath a journal that I kept there—a journal I consequently hadn't written in since someone gave it to me.

I picked up the letter. Turned it over. Looked at the seal.

It was still closed.

Unless someone had opened and resealed it.

But I didn't think that was the case.

My heart rate slowed.

Bryant didn't know what he was talking about.

But some of my worry now just turned into anger. I didn't want to work with that guy. I didn't want to support his projects.

There were so many red flags right now warning me that this could be a disaster that I wanted to run.

But I'd already signed on to do this.

Maybe I should contact my agent or attorney.

I wasn't sure.

But right now it was only three thirty. I still had a lot of the day left. A lot of time left that I could investigate.

Because for all I knew, tomorrow I might be back on the set.

Or by tomorrow, Shelby could be behind bars and this whole production could be on an indefinite pause.

I wasn't sure what was going to happen.

But I needed to make the most of my time right now.

I called an emergency meeting of the Hot Chicks along with Phoebe.

The Hot Chicks were a group of widows, each in their late sixties or early seventies, who had bonded after the deaths of their husbands. They were hysterical and loyal to each other and always there when I needed them.

Unfortunately, no one was available to meet until later tonight, so I had a few hours to kill until then. So I did what the next logical thing anyone in my shoes would do.

I went to the hospital to visit Kitty.

I knew she'd been shot and was in critical condition, but I didn't know exactly what that meant. Was she in a coma and unable to speak? Or was she suffering internal injuries that required round the clock monitoring?

I was going to find out.

A quiver of nerves swept through me as I stepped into The Outer Banks Hospital in Nags Head. But it wasn't as if this were my first rodeo. Since acting was what I did, I should be able to put on a good show.

I asked at the front desk to see her, and they gave me the room number. Then I took the elevator to the second floor and headed down the hallway.

Since she was in ICU, there was a good chance I wouldn't be able to visit her.

I was going to see what I could find out.

I headed into the waiting room and glanced around.

A man sat hunched forward in one of the seats. He had a buzz cut and a beard and mustache of the same color, all black mixed with strands of gray. I'd guess him to be close to Kitty's age.

I thought I'd heard somewhere that she was dating someone.

As the door closed behind me, the man looked up.

I paused a moment, not wanting to play with anyone's emotions.

Then I wandered toward the door in the waiting room that led to the ICU and hesitated in front of the call button.

"Who are you here to see?" the man asked.

I swallowed hard as I turned to him. "Kitty."

In a small hospital like this, there weren't many patients in intensive care, especially at this time of year.

He glanced at me as if sizing me up. "You a friend of hers?"

"Friend might be stretching it, but I heard what happened, and I wanted to check on her." That last part was the truth, at least.

"I'm Rick. Her boyfriend."

I swallowed hard. That was what I'd wondered.

The man seemed . . . off somehow. Like maybe he'd been drinking or he'd just taken a hit of something. Whatever his mental and physical state, he seemed talkative and friendly.

I didn't want to take advantage . . . but this could be the opportunity I'd been looking for.

I sat down in the seat near him, leaving ample space for comfort. "I'm really sorry to hear what happened."

"I just can't believe it." He hung his head as he shook it. "Still seems like a nightmare I can't wake up from."

"Were you there when it happened?"

"Yes. It happened at my place while I was sleeping in a bedroom on the other side of the house. I'd taken a sleeping pill, and I had the noise machine on. I've been having trouble sleeping lately, and it was starting to get to me. All that to say, I didn't hear anything." Guilt saturated each of his words.

My eyebrows shot up. "Oh, I see. Do you live in Manteo?"

"No, Nags Head."

The wheels continued to turn in my brain.

If the crime happened in Nags Head, that meant the Nags Head Police was covering this. Which meant . . . that maybe I *did* have a chance of getting some information from Jackson.

That idea shouldn't make my blood race, but it did.

I turned back to Rick. "How long have the two of you been together?"

"Six years."

I swallowed hard, trying to proceed carefully—and sympathetically. "I see. So you guys were together when . . . ?"

He nodded. "When Emma Jean died? Yes, and it was horrible."

"Did Emma Jean move back in with her mom when she came back to the area?"

"Oh, no. She and Kitty didn't get along. Emma Jean bought a place on the water. An old friend used to live there when she was in high school, and it was always her favorite house. When it went on the market . . . I suppose it felt fortuitous. And it was right down the street from where Andy Griffith used to live."

The actor was an icon in the area, and many liked to think of Manteo as a sort of real-life Mayberry.

"Who owns the house now?" I asked.

"It's been in probate. It should go to Kitty, but things have been more complicated than that."

"I know this is a weird question, but where were you and Kitty on the night Emma Jean died?"

"Kitty and I were in the mountains. In fact, we left the day before she died. I can't help but wonder if things would have been different if we were here." He shrugged. "Probably not. But I still wonder . . ."

Wait . . . if Kitty was out of town, then she couldn't be guilty.

My jaw hardened as I went back to the mental drawing board. Then I turned toward Rick. "Do you have any idea who did this to Kitty?"

His gaze hardened. "I know they have someone in custody. I haven't heard who."

"But it doesn't make sense," I continued. "*Why* would somebody do this?"

"That's what I keep asking myself as well. And I'm not sure."

"You said she was attacked at your house, though, right?" I clarified. "Someone said it happened at Kitty's place."

"Technically, it's my house. But Kitty bought it for me."

My breath caught. "She bought you a house?"

"She didn't want people to think she was money hungry, so she bought the house, said it was mine, and moved in."

"I guess she used the money Emma Jean gave her to do so?"

He nodded. "I guess. We've only owned it a few years."

My thoughts continued to race.

Maybe Kitty *did* arrange it so she would profit off her daughter's death. Did that mean she was a killer? Or that she'd hired someone to do her dirty work maybe?

I didn't know.

I still didn't even know if someone had killed Emma Jean.

I suppose that should be the first thing I tried to figure out. I still had a lot of work to do here.

But maybe the Hot Chicks could help me find answers.

chapter
twenty-four

I **WAS DRIVING** toward Dizzy's when my phone rang.

It was Isaac, *Ragdoll*'s assistant director. The man was in his mid-twenties and very driven. Total type A, but on the rare occasion he let down his guard, he was actually pretty fun.

His voice rang through the speaker in my car. "Joey . . ."

"Hey, Isaac."

"I'm calling everyone to give them an update. The cast and crew are having an emergency meeting in the morning, and it's essential that everyone be there."

An emergency meeting? That didn't sound good.

"What's the meeting about?" I stared at the road in front of me.

"About the future of this production. Things just got a whole lot more complicated."

My mind raced with possibilities . . . "What do you mean?"

He sighed. "I'd like to just tell everyone in the morning so I don't have to repeat myself one million times."

"You can tell me since we're already talking, can't you?"

Isaac let out another sigh. "The truth is, Selby is being held at the station."

I sucked in a breath. "Is that right? I knew the police took him in for questioning, but I thought that was just a formality."

"Between you and me, he and Kitty had an altercation last night."

Maggie had mentioned that also. But I wondered if Isaac knew what it was about.

I swallowed hard. "An altercation?"

"That's right. Selby tried to get Kitty to see things his way. Kitty wouldn't have anything to do with it. She didn't want the movie to be made. Things got pretty heated."

Selby was looking guiltier all the time.

Yet I knew he was the kind of guy who really liked to think things through, who didn't act on impulse.

For that reason, I had a hard time picturing him pulling a gun and firing.

"That's all I want to say about it now," Isaac said. "But, hopefully, I'll have more information in the morning, and we can go from there. Okay?"

"Of course," I told him. "I'll be there with bells on."

With bells on? Come on, Joey. You can do better than that.

The only bells I needed to be worried about were those alarm bells going off in my head as I wondered what danger I might run into next.

I pulled up to Dizzy's house—she insisted we'd have more privacy there.

The rest of the Hot Chicks, as well as Phoebe, had already arrived and greeted me when I stepped inside.

Dizzy was their fearless leader.

Maxine owned a wonderful second-hand store called Utter Clutter.

Geraldine was a gentle soul who'd been a homemaker.

MaryAnn was a retired schoolteacher and the mother of Officer Loose Lips.

Dizzy had put together a vegetable tray, a cheeseball with crackers, some pimento cheese sandwiches cut into triangles, and she'd made some punch with sherbet, juice, and Sprite.

I had the Hot Chicks' rapt attention as they all sat around me, and I filled them in on everything.

Then the questions came from every side.

What did Kitty spend the life insurance policy money on?

What was Kitty's altercation with Selby about? Could he have shot her?

Why was Maverick such a jerk to you? What is he hiding?

How is Cyrus staying afloat in a brick-and-mortar store in today's economy?

How did Emma Jean and Todd strike up that unlikely friendship?

Was Bobbi really telling the truth?

They were all valid questions—questions I didn't have the answers to.

But it all went back to my earlier doubt about whether this was all a crazy hunch or not.

"Before I go down this rabbit hole, I really need to figure out if Emma Jean was truly murdered or not," I murmured. "Some people *do* have motives. But if her death truly was an accident, then I'm wasting all this time for no good reason."

"Then what's the best way to find that out?" Dizzy

plucked a piece of celery from the vegetable tray at the center of the table and dunked it into the ranch dressing.

I thought through her question a moment. "I suppose there's the autopsy, although it sounded like the results from it weren't questioned five years ago."

"I don't suppose there were any witnesses," Maxine murmured. "At least, none that we know about."

"Maybe there's someone out there who saw something but hasn't come forward," MaryAnn said.

"Maybe," I murmured.

"It sounds like you've already traced Emma Jean's final steps from when she bought that medicine to when she headed back to her house and . . . didn't quite make it." Geraldine, the more subtle type, grabbed a carrot and gently plunged it into some ranch dressing.

I leaned back in my chair. "Maybe it's impossible to prove that she was murdered. Maybe I'm chasing the wind and I'll never have any answers."

Dizzy leaned closer, a motherly look suddenly filling her gaze. "I'm afraid if you don't have any answers then you're never going to be at peace doing this biopic."

She had a point.

It bothered me that the details didn't feel accurate.

Bryant's portrayal of me in the manuscript I'd stumbled upon also bothered me. I truly didn't want to support anything his name was on.

I'd told the ladies part of that story too, and they'd rightfully called him a dog.

The sad truth was that he could get that book published even if his facts weren't accurate.

Then I supposed I could sue him for libel.

The thing with Emma Jean was that she was dead by the time her story came out. She didn't have the chance to defend herself.

"So what do we do now?" Dizzy asked.

Before I could answer that question, my phone beeped.

When I looked at the screen, I saw that the alarm at my rental house was going off . . . again.

IRRITATION WASHED through me as I murmured, "Excuse me a minute."

All these little emergencies Ezra was having were driving me nuts.

I paced away from the group and called the alarm company again. They gave me a new code I'd need to turn the alarm off.

Then I tried to call Ezra. But he didn't answer. Of *course.*

My irritation grew deeper by the moment. Just what was going on with this guy?

I returned to the rest of the group, and they each looked up at me with hopeful expressions. I told them what was going on.

"So what are you going to do?" Phoebe tucked her legs beneath her while nibbling on a carrot.

I let my head drop back against the couch, fighting exasperation. "I wish I could ignore the whole situation and that would make it go away."

"Maybe you should let that alarm go off," Dizzy said. "Let it annoy your little renter dude for a while."

That was *one* idea . . .

As if on cue, my phone rang. Ezra?

I glanced at the screen and frowned.

Nope, it was Ms. Robinson. I quickly answered, not bothering to move off the couch this time.

"Can you please turn that alarm off?" she asked, her voice scratchier and more high-pitched than usual. "It's driving me bonkers."

I guess that solved that. No, I couldn't ignore it.

"I'll get right on it," I promised her.

I put my phone back in my pocket and frowned at the ladies around me.

"Unfortunately, the alarm isn't bothering my renter, but it *is* bothering the neighbor."

"What are you going to do?" Dizzy asked.

MaryAnn gave me a motherly look. "You can't go over there by yourself, Joey. You know that, don't you?"

"I'm not planning on doing that. The police have been notified, but I'm going to call your son and see if he can personally check things out. He knows a little about what's going on, so I'd feel better if he went."

It had nothing to do with the fact that he would probably give me more details on Ezra than any of the other officers.

The choice seemed awfully responsible to me.

I gave myself a mental pat on the back.

And that was exactly what I did. I called Officer Loose Lips, who promised to head right over.

I was playing it safe and proud of myself for doing so.

Phoebe came home with me, bless her heart. First, we'd picked up her dog from her place and then we headed to my house.

I was eternally grateful for her because I didn't want to stay at my place again by myself.

On the drive back, I'd tried to call Danny for an update, but he hadn't answered.

Which I found weird. But maybe he was in the middle of something. It wasn't as if Jackson could always answer my calls either, especially if he was working on something important.

Once inside with the doors locked, my phone rang.

It was Jackson.

I wondered if he had any updates for me.

I excused myself from Phoebe and slipped into my room.

"What's new?" I started.

"I figured you'd want to know that the police are looking at security footage from businesses around the area to figure out what happened to Kitty."

It was like the man could read my mind. "Were there any cameras at the house?"

"According to the boyfriend, they talked about having them installed but never did." Jackson let out a long breath. "Anyway, I know they have a suspect in custody, but they're still investigating. Nothing appeared to be stolen from the home, however."

"You said, 'a suspect'?" Yes, I was fishing for information.

"I can't give you a name. I'm sorry."

I frowned but didn't push him anymore. I was trying to learn my limits and when to push them and when to pull back. Right now, I decided to wait.

Instead, I huddled on a cozy blue chair in the corner and gave him the update on what happened at the rental house.

"I don't like that all of this is happening." Jackson's tone tightened protectively.

I had to admit that I loved that about him. Some women were all independent and stuff, but I liked knowing that someone was looking out for me.

"I don't either. But I sent Danny over there. However, he hasn't called me back yet. I was hoping for an update."

Jackson grunted. "I'll see if he'll answer for me. I'm sure he's probably just busy."

"That's what I assumed also." Although several scenarios had played out in my head.

We talked for a few more minutes before saying I love you and getting off the phone.

As I put my phone away, I quickly glanced out my window at the sidewalk running in front of my house.

I fully expected to see the man with a cigarette out there.

But I saw nothing.

Maybe it was all a coincidence.

I only hoped if it *wasn't* a coincidence that the person who'd been out there was long gone now.

chapter
twenty-six

I HAD JUST DRIFTED to sleep when my phone rang.

At least, I *thought* I'd just drifted to sleep.

I plucked one eye open and saw it was one-thirty a.m.

Who would call me at one-thirty in the morning?

Then I saw a name on the screen.

Hubba Hubba Hubby.

If Jackson was calling me at this hour, then something was wrong.

I quickly answered, my thoughts already racing. "Jackson . . . what's going on?"

"Sorry to wake you, sweetheart. But Danny has disappeared."

"What?" My throat tightened. "What do you mean *disappeared?*"

"I mean that after he went to our house, he went radio silent. No one has heard from him since then."

My head dropped back into my pillow. "Are you serious?"

"Dead."

I knew Jackson hadn't used that word on accident.

"What could have happened to him?"

"Sono went to our rental house, but no one was there. It looked like no one was ever there."

I remembered the trash bags. The rope.

My heart raced, and I sat up. "Is Danny's police car still there?"

"That's the other weird thing. It is. But Danny is nowhere to be seen."

My heart thumped harder. "What about Ms. Robinson? Did they question her and see if she'd seen anything?"

"Apparently, she got annoyed by the chirping of the alarm, and she closed her blinds and turned up the Hallmark movie she was watching on TV. She didn't hear or see anything."

I nibbled on my bottom lip. "That's unfortunate."

"Sono wants to question you. I need to know everything you know about the guy who was staying there or anything that Danny may have said."

"Of course. Whatever I can do to help."

"Don't answer the door for anybody except for Detective Sono, understand?"

"Of course."

What could have happened to Danny?

And what if this somehow was associated with that Ezra guy?

Detective Sono had come to my place last night after I talked to Jackson. I'd told him everything I knew about my renter. He hadn't given me any additional information on Officer Danny. I only knew he was still missing.

I felt terribly for MaryAnn and what she must be going through.

I couldn't help but think it was partially my fault. After all, I'd called the police and sent Danny to a house I owned, knowing good and well how creepy the man inside was. But I figured Danny could handle it.

What if I'd been wrong?

When Detective Sono and I finished that conversation, part of me wanted to ask him about Selby. But it seemed inconsiderate given the fact that an officer was missing, so I didn't. Plus, Serious Sono didn't seem very chatty.

Phoebe had woken up and lingered nearby as everything went down.

After Detective Sono left, my mind raced at full speed, and I was unable to fall back to sleep.

That meant that today would be a very long day.

At four-thirty, I'd finally given in and made some coffee. Then Phoebe and I had filled ourselves up with caffeine, watched some *Grey's Anatomy* reruns, and chatted.

By the time eight a.m. hit, I still hadn't heard anything. My meeting with Isaac and the rest of the casting crew was coming up soon.

I had no idea what might transpire with that either.

I also wondered about Kitty and if there were any updates on her.

I had so many threads dangling in front of me that I felt like a fish trying to decide which fishing line and bait was safe—but unlike the fish, I knew none of them were truly safe.

Phoebe went into work bright and early at Oh Buoy, and I also got dressed and headed out to the house where we were supposed to be filming.

A lot of actors and crew were already there with coffee in hand. Half looked tired, and the other half looked curious.

Bryant was there also.

I tried not to scowl at the man.

I wasn't supposed to know about that manuscript he'd written. If I did let on that I knew then he'd know I'd been in his room.

I needed to figure out how to handle that at some point.

But for now, I took my place in a little semi-circle, and I watched as Isaac got everyone's attention.

"I hate to be the one to be the bearer of bad news," he began. "However, as I'm sure most of you know already, Selby has been charged in the shooting of Kitty Gibbons."

Murmurs raced through the cast and crew.

"Production has been postponed until we can get more clarity on this," Isaac continued.

"What are we supposed to do in the meantime?" Maggie asked.

"We're asking for everyone to stick around until the end of the week. We hope to make a decision by then."

More murmuring and questions began.

Once people began to disperse, Isaac turned toward me. That was when I saw the weariness in his gaze.

Though on the outside he seemed to be handling this well, this was all taking a toll on him.

"I heard you've solved some real-life crimes," he started.

"I have . . ." I wondered where he was going with this.

"Can you look into this? I can slip you some money . . ."

"I'm not too concerned about money."

"But will you do it?" His gaze latched onto mine.

I only had to consider it for a moment. "Of course I will."

A relieved smile stretched across his face. "Good. Because if the charges against Selby stick, then the production is doomed."

twenty-seven

AFTER ISAAC WRAPPED up the meeting, most of the cast and crew stuck around chatting among themselves.

I lingered close also, waiting for someone to say something interesting. But all I heard was concern. Questions about whether people would stay or go and what this meant for the production.

Could Selby really be guilty?

No one knew, nor did anyone really have anything noteworthy to say.

But when I saw Maggie slip away, I had to wonder where she was going.

Why would she leave so quietly? It didn't seem like her.

I knew I shouldn't take action, but when had that ever stopped me before?

I slipped away and followed her.

I couldn't exactly be stealthy in my red Miata, but I'd do my best to maintain a healthy distance behind her.

I was surprised when several minutes later she pulled up to Orbitz.

I found a parking space and climbed out, casually getting closer so I could catch a glimpse of what she might be doing.

She and Cyrus were talking inside—and the conversation appeared animated.

Strange.

As she turned and stormed toward the door, I stashed myself beside the building.

The door slammed open, and I caught sight of her heading toward the inn.

What had that been about?

What reason would Maggie have for talking to Cyrus? For arguing with him?

I wasn't sure. But I needed to find out.

When I climbed back into my car, my phone rang. It was Jackson. He must be on a break.

I answered with, "Do you have an update on Danny?"

He'd been on my mind all morning. I wanted to do something to help him, but I didn't know what. I also knew that every officer in the area was going to be on this.

"We still haven't been able to find him," Jackson said. "No leads either."

"Do you think it's foul play?"

"We're not sure. But we did trace this Ezra guy's credit cards, and it turns out he recently bought some rope and trash bags."

My throat suddenly went dry. I had seen those things.

"And Izzes," I murmured before I realized what I was saying.

"What?"

"Nothing."

"Joey . . . I heard you say something."

I let out an aggravated breath—aggravated at myself. "I saw some Izzes along with the rope and trash bags when I went to the house."

"You didn't mention that to me."

"I thought it was a coincidence. Other people than me like Izzes."

"Sounds like this guy is up to something."

"I guess you haven't been able to find him yet either?"

"No, he's in the wind."

"I haven't been able to stop thinking about it. If there's anything I can do . . ."

"Just take care of MaryAnn. That's all. The police can handle the rest."

I bit back a frown. "Got it."

"Now, there's something else that I wanted to mention to you."

I braced myself. Would this be good news or bad news? I had no idea what to expect.

"I talked to Raymond Kent. He's the new medical examiner in the area."

"And?"

"He wasn't working in this area when Emma Jean died. But he has the files on her death and said he would be willing to review them."

"What?" I sat up. "Really?"

"Really. And he's a big fan of yours so he's hoping you might stop by to go through things with him."

Jackson's words made me pause. "He's not creepy or anything, is he?"

"No, he's a good guy. Very personable. Very funny. I wouldn't tell you to meet with him one-on-one if I didn't trust him."

My shoulders loosened. Good. So much had happened that it had me on edge sometimes.

"When does he want to meet?" I asked.

"He wanted to know how soon you were available."

"I'm available . . . now."

"I'll let him know."

A grin tugged at my lips.

Maybe things were starting to look up.

Maybe.

BEFORE I HEADED to the police station to meet with Raymond, I called Dizzy.

She'd closed early for the day and was with MaryAnn and the rest of the Hot Chicks. When hard times hit, they came together. That was the beauty of friendship.

As expected, MaryAnn wasn't holding up well. I wouldn't expect anyone in her position to, however.

"Is there anything I can do for her?" I stared at my kitchen and considered making her food. On second thought, she'd be better off if I ordered something for her.

"Figure out where Danny is." Dizzy sounded dead serious. "Please."

She was the second person in less than an hour to ask for my help.

I was flattered.

And, of course, I wanted to do whatever I could.

I had solved a few cases before. Some of them had simply been luck. But there were others where I'd used the skills I had learned as a first-class detective in *Relentless.*

"I'm going to do whatever I can to find out information on what happened to Danny," I said. "He was at my rental when it happened. But I'm sure you know that."

"Do you think the person staying there did something?" Dizzy asked.

I remembered Ezra and repressed a shiver. "He was kind of creepy, but I thought I was his target, not a cop. I guess I really don't know right now."

"Please, help him. Please." Desperation tinged her voice.

"I'll do everything that I can."

Then I ended the call and headed out to meet with the medical examiner.

Raymond Kent was in his forties, mostly bald, and thin. He seemed enthusiastic but harmless. And he clearly loved solving crimes and everything scientific.

I could admire that.

We met at his office at the police station. His full-time job was as a family doctor in Nags Head, but he had his own space here when he needed it.

"I thought it was fascinating that you wanted to see the autopsy reports on Emma Jean," he told me as he sat across the desk with files in front of him. "Thankfully, the records aren't sealed so I was able to legally access it and study it."

"That's good news, at least." I crossed and recrossed my legs, anxious to hear his thoughts—but not wanting to seem impatient, even though I was.

"I know that everyone says her death was accidental. But there were some very interesting things that I noted in these reports, starting with the skull fracture."

I liked where he was going with this so far. "What about it?"

He showed me some images of a skull. "You can see the injury right here on the left of the frontal cortex. So there is a slight chance she could have fallen and hit her head on one of the railings on the bridge."

"Did they look at the bridge for evidence to see if she did indeed do that? Was there blood or something else left there?" Why hadn't I thought to ask that sooner?

His eyes lit. "That's a most excellent question. As far as I know, they didn't find anything. However, making it more complicated is the fact that it was raining that night."

"But you think it's a plausible scenario?" I asked. "That this truly could be an accident?"

"Maybe. Maybe not. And I know that doesn't sound very definitive, but let me explain. I was trying to imagine what could have happened and to recreate the scene in my mind. If Ms. Gibbons fell from the bike and hit her head on the bridge, I'd expect her to have hit the bridge somewhere in this area." He circled an area toward the side of the skull. "For her to hit where the fracture occurred, well . . . it's not entirely impossible, but it's not likely either."

"Okay . . ." I was trying to read between the lines, which was always dangerous.

"Plus, this fracture shows that it was a direct hit." He pointed to the X-ray again. "You can tell by the way the bone is broken and due to the fact it's near the front of her face. It almost makes me wonder if someone hit her with something."

"Right . . ."

"Would you mind standing?"

"Sure . . ." I wasn't sure where he was going with this.

He eyed me a moment. "You're about the same height as she was. If a man approximately my size—I'm five eleven—were to swing something at you, it would hit at this approximate location."

He demonstrated on me how that would have worked using an imaginary stick.

"That's what I've seen most often when someone has been beaten," he continued.

I shivered. I didn't like the sound of that, but at least we were making some progress.

"That is very interesting." But I wasn't sure I was any closer to answers right now.

"The blow to the head isn't what killed her," Raymond said. "But it did cause her most likely to pass out and fall into the water, where she drowned."

Or someone left her there to die. I kept that part to myself.

"There's something else that I found interesting." He sat back down and motioned for me to do the same.

I lowered myself into the chair.

"Something else?" I couldn't wait to hear what, especially if it meant finding answers.

RAYMOND HAD MORE energy than I did, *and* he talked faster than I did. I wasn't sure if I should be overwhelmed or jealous.

"I know they examined all this evidence when they conducted her death investigation," he continued. "But something about this bike tire strikes me as strange."

I squinted as I studied the photo he pulled out, trying to see what he saw.

"The thing is, I'm a biker. I know bikes, and I've been in a few accidents myself. When I look at that tire it doesn't strike me as one that hit something, making Ms. Gibbons topple off, hit her head, and then fall into the marsh."

I studied it closer. "You can tell that by looking at this photo?"

His eyes gleamed with a little pride. "There have been many studies done about the impact of crashes on bicycles. But right now I'm mostly speaking from personal experience. I was in an accident once where my front tire hit a guardrail, kind of similar to what happened to Ms. Gibbons. There was clearly a dent in the rim when that happened. The tire also popped off."

"So what's so strange about Emma Jean's?" I was trying to follow where he was going with this. But he talked so fast it was hard to keep up.

"What's strange about it is that there are actually two dents."

I squinted as I continued to study the photo. Now that Raymond had brought it up, I could see what he was talking about.

"What do you think caused that?" I asked.

He beamed even brighter. "I'm glad you asked. Because you remember that earlier theory I told you about? That maybe someone could have hit her on the head, maybe with a bat or something?"

"Yes?"

"What if . . . someone asked her to meet out there at the bridge? Then this person hit Ms. Gibbons with the bat and knew they needed to cover up the crime. So after she was in the water, the killer took their bat and hit the tire. But the first hit didn't work, so this person had to hit the tire again. But what if the killer hit the bike again at a slightly different space? That would have caused these two dents."

I leaned back in my chair. I had to admit I was impressed.

"This is all off the record." Raymond peered at me over the top of his glasses.

"Of course. I appreciate you sitting down and sharing your theories with me."

"I love stuff like this." He shifted in his seat. "There was one other detail I noticed. Ms. Gibbons had a check in her pocket, which I found odd. That information hasn't been released to the public. If anyone finds out, I'll know it was you."

"I won't share. But why is that odd?"

"She's biking with nothing else in her pockets except some pills and a check? And the check and pill bottle stayed in her pocket while her suicide note flew out? It just doesn't fit."

"I agree." He made an excellent point.

"If you think Ms. Gibbons was murdered, I'd say there was a good chance you're right. If I'd been the medical examiner when this had happened, I wouldn't have closed the case so easily. That's not to say that the previous medical examiner didn't do his job. He did. He had no reason to suspect someone might have harmed her on purpose. But I'd say it's something worth exploring for sure."

I loved hearing his justification of my suspicions entirely more than I should. "So, if I'm hearing you right, this person had to be strong enough to hit her with a bat or something similar and crack her skull. Also, the killer would probably be someone Emma Jean knew since she was meeting this person at the bridge."

"I very seriously doubt it was a random stranger who did this."

"Do you think it could have been a woman?"

He made a face. "It seems highly unlikely. There was quite a bit of force to that blow to the head. Plus, a woman would have been shorter than a man, making the fracture different. It's only speculation, but my bet would be on a man."

I chewed on my thumbnail as I let that sink in, and then I nodded. "Thank you so much for your time."

He stood and extended his hand, a bright smile on his face. "No problem. Anytime."

Anytime?

He had no idea what he'd just said.

Before I left the police station, I paused at the front desk. It just so happened that Detective Sono walked past as I stood there.

He paused, and I could see the irritation in his gaze. Despite that, he plastered on a smile.

"How's it going, Joey?"

He was only being nice to me because of Jackson. I knew that.

"It's going," I told him. "Any updates on Danny you can tell me about?"

He shook his head. "Not yet. But we're trying to track his phone. We're hopeful we might find him that way."

"I hope so. I hate that this happened."

"We all do."

I paused and shifted. "Listen, the director for the movie I'm working on is behind bars."

His gaze darkened. "I'm well aware."

"What are the chances I could talk to him?"

He gave me a sour look. "Are you his lawyer?"

I tilted my head and gave him a sour look right back. "I think you know the answer to that. I did play one on TV one time, though."

He rolled his eyes. "That doesn't count."

"Certainly other people can see Selby besides a lawyer. What if he was married and his wife wanted to see him?"

"Are you his wife?"

Now I was getting annoyed. Sono was just being a smart mouth.

"Look, is there any way I could talk to him?"

He stared at me a moment as if he wanted to just slam some sort of mental door in my face.

But finally, he stepped back from the counter. "Let me see what I can do."

I held my breath as I waited to see what he would say.

thirty

I **WASN'T** sure who was more surprised—me or Detective Sono—when he returned and told me I had permission from the chief to talk to Selby.

Chief Lawson had always liked me. I'd done some PR work for the department when I'd first moved to this area, tweeting about their accomplishments.

I'd also donated to some important causes. Not that I wanted to use that to my advantage. But if it happened to work out like that, who was I to argue?

"Right this way." Sono nodded for me to follow.

He went through the door leading into the secure area in the back and had nearly let it shut behind him before I caught up with him—just in time to grab the door before it locked me out.

He was going to report all this back to Jackson. It wasn't a question.

I had no doubt that would be the case. But I didn't let that stop me right now.

He led me into a room—I'd seen it many times before—where Selby was now sitting. They must have just pulled him out of the small cell here at the station.

Selby looked terrible. Pale with deep circles under his bloodshot eyes.

The man was clearly under a lot of stress—as anyone would be in the situation.

"Joey . . . glad that you came." His words sounded listless, however, with no hint of gladness.

"I imagine you've had lots of visitors."

He shook his head. "You think people want to be affiliated with someone accused of shooting a woman?"

"Why do they think you shot Kitty?" I cautiously dropped in the seat across from him.

He let out a long, burdened breath. "I heard Kitty lived with her boyfriend, so I went to his house that night, hoping to catch her. I did and, as usual, she was furious from the moment she laid eyes on me. Our little talk turned into an argument. But I didn't shoot her."

"What was your argument about?"

He ran a hand through his hair. "I really wanted us to be on the same page as far as this movie. I didn't want all of the stress and drama of a lawsuit. I knew she could make things ugly."

"Which consequently also gives you a motive to be the assailant."

He hung his head. "I know. Believe me, I know."

"I'm assuming you have a lawyer?"

"I do. My attorney in California recommended someone who lives in Raleigh. He drove in last night to represent me."

"I'm assuming this guy is looking into this and trying to figure out who else could have done it?"

"Of course he is. He suspects some guy named Cyrus might be behind it."

"Cyrus? The guy who owns the music store?" I tried to keep the surprise from my voice but failed.

He raised an eyebrow. "You know him?"

I shrugged. "Kind of. Why would he attack Kitty?"

"Apparently, Cyrus thinks Kitty has the power to give him royalties on that song. He's been coming after her for years to get more money."

"You really think Cyrus would have taken it that far?"

"I have no idea. But I'm all out of other explanations. I only know I didn't shoot Kitty. You've got to help me, Joey."

Selby pleaded with me with his gaze—something I never thought I'd see him do. He was usually so self-assured and non-emotional. But panic could affect people in different ways.

What was it with people asking me to help them?

I wasn't sure. But I appeared to be in demand.

I only hoped I didn't let everyone down.

As I left the station, there was only one other place I wanted to go.

I wanted to see the house Emma Jean had purchased when she moved back to this area.

The one that was right down the street from Andy Griffith's.

It wasn't too hard to find the address online. Though it wasn't public, enough of her fans had posted clues that I knew I'd find it.

As I headed down the road back toward Manteo, I glanced in my rearview mirror.

A dark sedan with dark-tinted windows followed behind me.

Vehicles with tinted windows always seemed to be trouble.

I wanted to believe I was seeing things that weren't actually there, but I couldn't.

Because every turn I made, that car turned also.

I tried to catch a glimpse of the license plate, but I couldn't make out the letters and numbers there.

I gripped the wheel harder.

To test the waters, I made a sudden left turn and headed away from Manteo.

I glanced in my rearview mirror. This would be the true test to see if this person was following me or not.

I didn't see the other driver for a couple of seconds.

Then the car appeared again.

My heart sped.

I had to think of a way to lose this guy.

If Emma Jean truly was murdered, her killer could fear I was getting too close to the truth.

He could try to silence me, just like he'd tried to silence Kitty.

I had to ask myself WWJD: What Would Jackson Do?

Other times, the J stood for Jesus. And it still did, in a way.

But I needed to think like Jackson right now if I wanted to get out of this alive.

I glanced around again, my mind racing.

Then I found my answer.

I quickly pulled into an empty driveway located under a house. Both sides of the space had wooden trellises to conceal the area.

As soon as I parked, I grabbed the two trashcans at

the side of the house and pulled them behind my car to block it from sight.

Then I waited. If my plan worked, I should be able to get away.

But I also realized if my plan failed, I'd be in a very sticky situation.

A FEW MINUTES LATER, the car passed.

I released the air from my lungs. But it was too soon to assume I was safe.

Instead, I waited another couple of minutes to see if the driver turned around to find me.

I didn't see him.

Maybe the coast really was clear.

I hesitated another moment before moving the trashcans back into place and backing out.

Then I headed out on the street, still glancing around to see if I could put my eyes on that vehicle again.

But I didn't see it.

Finally, I turned back onto the main highway and headed toward Manteo.

Several minutes later, I pulled down a long, gravel

lane that ended at a white colonial-style house located on the Roanoke Sound.

I parked and climbed out, trying to be cautious.

I scurried past the house toward the water.

Cyrus said that this was where Emma Jean liked to write her music, and I could see why.

A bench swing hung from a live oak near the water. I tested it before sitting there.

Using my toes, I swung myself back and forth as I stared over the placid Roanoke Sound. I imagined Emma Jean doing this very thing.

I pictured her sitting here with her guitar and that leather-bound journal that she liked to sketch her notes in.

What had happened to that journal? According to Todd, she'd been out here working on some new music the very day she died.

"Emma Jean, what did you do with whatever you wrote that day?" I looked at the sky as if she might answer.

Of course, there was only silence.

So I closed my eyes again and pictured her here jotting down ideas.

What if in the middle of her writing process something startled her? What if she decided to leave right then?

Where would she have put her notebook?

I knew it was a longshot.

But I glanced around anyway.

What if she had stashed it somewhere out here? If she had a hiding place where she thought no one would find it? Most people would have looked inside. But maybe inside was too obvious, especially if she didn't trust people.

Was my theory crazy?

Maybe.

But I decided to look anyway.

I'd spent the last ten minutes looking in hollow logs in the woods. Along the deck. Near a picnic table.

Really, I felt silly. I knew my theory was far-fetched.

Yet I couldn't stop myself from looking either.

Maybe Emma Jean had put it somewhere else.

Maybe that journal wasn't even important.

Yet another part of me imagined her writing on those pages about any angst she was experiencing. It had probably been therapeutic.

In fact, that journal might even have the answers we needed to find her killer.

I glanced around one more time.

But, really, there was nowhere else out here she

could have stashed the journal. No place where the weather, after all these years, wouldn't have gotten to it.

I started back to my car. I hadn't accomplished much except talking to a deceased Emma Jean.

But at least now I had a better feel of this place she loved.

Halfway back to my car, I paused by an outdoor stone fireplace.

One of her songs had referenced fire by the water. What were those lyrics? Something about it was a place where secrets were laid.

I nibbled on my lip a moment.

Another longshot, but . . .

Could she have stashed her journal here?

The idea almost sounded ridiculous. But what if it wasn't?

Musicians held close to their music like some people would a valuable treasure. Maybe she felt threatened, like someone would steal her lyrics.

But where on this fireplace would Emma Jean hide something that would have survived the elements?

I stared at the stone chimney a moment, my thoughts racing.

There was only one place that made sense.

I touched the hearth. It was a big, solid slab of stone that covered the entire front of the fireplace.

And it was loose.

My throat tightened.

I drew in a hesitant breath before lifting the corner of the slab.

I had little confidence I'd find anything inside.

But those lyrics I'd read just kept coming back to me.

As I peered beneath the stone, my breath caught.

Something leather grabbed my attention.

Something that looked like a journal.

I released the air from my lungs.

It looked like my gut instinct was right after all.

AS SOON AS I got back into my car, I couldn't wait to look through Emma Jean's journal. Yet staying here at her house felt too risky.

I needed to go somewhere private.

Just in case someone was watching me.

But was there anywhere truly private?

On second thought, maybe going somewhere public would be my best bet.

For that reason, I drove to the drugstore.

I didn't go inside. But I parked at the front of the building, right within view of a security camera.

Then I opened that journal.

My heart pounded in my ears.

Emma Jean had definitely been working on some new songs.

And they were good. I could easily see the catchy lyrics taking off.

Instead of reading every song, I skipped to the last page, where I assumed her most recent song would be.

The words at the top read "The Death of Me."

My throat went dry.

Would this song provide the answers I was looking for?

I can feel you chasing me,
Wanting a piece of me.
You'll be the death of me.
I want to look away,
To run away,
To get away,
But there's no way to escape.
Only to reshape.
To find the strength to remaster the final tape.

Then the bridge:

I'm staring death in the face.
Is this my fate?
It takes my breath away.
It wasn't supposed to be this way.
I'm so helpless,
And so afraid.

I thought I'd paid.
But you're still chasing me . . .
This is the way it's going to be.
You're going to be the death of me.

My thoughts raced.

Emma Jean definitely sounded fearful.

Sounded like she felt something terrible closing in on her. Felt desperate even, like maybe someone was threatening her.

But the one thing she didn't include was who she'd been afraid of.

I had a suspect in my mind.

One person who made sense.

For that reason, I headed back to Orbitz.

I walked into Orbitz and saw just the person I wanted to speak to behind the counter.

Cyrus Pitts.

He paused when he saw me come in. But this time, he was onto me. He was no longer the naive music store owner who had no idea who I was or what I was up to.

He crossed his arms. "Mrs. Darling. What brings you in this time?"

"I'm just going to cut to the chase." I stopped near the counter, resisting the urge to sing along with Shania Twain as she belted out a tune about feeling like a woman. "I think someone murdered Emma Jean and tried to make it look like an accident."

Cyrus tilted his head, unaffected by my words. "Okay . . . that still doesn't tell me why you're in here."

"I'm in here because you're my number one suspect."

His eyes widened and then he suddenly dropped his arms, taking a step back. "Whoa, whoa, whoa. I didn't kill Emma Jean."

"Everyone knows you hated her because she stole that song from you and she never gave you credit."

"That much is true. I do harbor a lot of hard feelings. But anyone in my shoes would."

I leveled my gaze at him. "Perhaps it made you hate her enough that you wanted to kill her."

He quickly—adamantly—shook his head. "No. I'm not the murderous type."

I leaned closer. "Then what type are you?"

He stared at me a moment, and I waited for his answer.

Maybe this was where I'd get my confession.

chapter
thirty-three

"I'M the type of person who will sell my soul rather at the cost of justice," Cyrus announced.

"What?" His words didn't make any sense.

"I'm the type of person who will sell my soul at the cost of justice." He raised his chin as if he were offering an acceptance speech.

"I know," I murmured. "You said that already. But it didn't make any more sense the second time."

"I'm trying out the lyrics for a new song I'm writing." He shook his head as if my statement had thrown him off track. "What I meant was that the record company offered me a secret deal if I kept my mouth shut."

"A secret deal?" I stared at him, wondering exactly where he was going with this.

"They said they'd give me a nice chunk of money to keep my mouth shut and not take them to court. At first, I wasn't going to accept the offer. Then I realized I'd be a fool not to. So I took the deal."

"How much did they give you?"

He smirked. "Let's just say it was more than a million."

I nodded slowly. "That's a nice chunk of change."

"It's the only reason I've been able to keep this store open," he admitted. "It certainly doesn't pay for itself."

Things were beginning to make more sense.

But if Cyrus had been paid off, what sense would it make to kill Emma Jean? What would his motive be?

Maybe he wasn't guilty like I thought he was.

For some reason, that disappointed me. I wasn't saying I wanted the man to be a killer. But if not Cyrus, then who?

As if on cue, the door opened.

And someone else I wanted to question stepped inside.

Maggie O'Peters paused in the doorway when she saw me. "Joey? What are *you* doing here?"

"What are *you* doing here?" I echoed back to her.

I had pretty much ruled Maggie out as a suspect since there were no indications she'd been in town at the time Emma Jean was murdered. Nor did the two women have any prior connection.

So why had Maggie been talking to Cyrus yesterday?

I felt certain the woman was hiding something.

"I'm just here to talk to Cyrus." Maggie nodded behind me at the man.

"I wasn't aware that the two if you knew each other," I continued.

Maggie stepped closer. "We don't. But I happened to wander in here the other day, and he has a first edition of a Rolling Stones album that I have been trying to find for years. I'm going to buy it for my husband for his birthday. He'll love it."

Cyrus reached below the counter before displaying the album she'd spoken of. "It's right here."

Maggie stepped closer, shaking her head in awe as she stared at it. Moisture filled her eyes, and she placed a hand over her heart. "It's just beautiful."

"I think so too." Cyrus practically beamed. "I'm happy to sell it to someone who will appreciate it."

Well, I guess that cleared that up.

And that meant I was right back to square one.

Who had killed Emma Jean Gibbons?
Not Cyrus.
Not Maggie.
Who else did that leave?

chapter
thirty-four

I **FELT** like a dog with its tail between its legs as I left Orbitz.

I really needed to narrow the suspects down to people who would have been in Manteo and known Emma Jean back then. That was the key.

That mostly left locals. Kitty might still be a possibility, although Rick said the two of them were out of town. I could only assume the police had double-checked their alibis.

I suppose there was Maverick, maybe even Todd.

I wasn't sure.

Then there was that check that Raymond had mentioned finding in Emma Jean's pocket. Whoever it had been written out to had been smeared and illegible.

Was that check in any way significant?

It seemed like it might be.

Before I took off down the road, my phone dinged.

The alarm at my rental house was going off. Again.

I let my head drop back into my seat in exasperation.

This renter was going to be the death of me.

Then I remembered that Danny was missing.

And if that alarm had gone off . . . what if that meant that Ezra was there? And what if Ezra had answers as to what had happened to Danny?

I quickly called Detective Sono and told him what was going on. He promised to get to my house right away.

But there was no way I was just going to stay here and do nothing while he investigated.

I needed answers also. I felt personally responsible for what had happened to Danny. I was the one who'd sent him over there, after all. And his poor mother . . . I knew she was so worried.

For that reason, I put my car into Drive and took off.

When I arrived at the rental, there was already a police cruiser outside.

Trying to be smart, I remained where I was and watched.

At once, I heard a commotion inside the house. Almost like there was a fight or a struggle. Things banged around. Footsteps hit the floor, shaking the house.

What was going on in there?

If Ezra had hurt Danny, who was to say he wouldn't hurt Detective Sono?

Did the detective have backup? Or was he in there alone?

I held my breath as I tried to figure out what to do.

Finally, I realized I couldn't wait a moment longer.

I had to figure out if Sono was okay.

I quickly texted a couple of the other officers I knew.

But they wouldn't get there before I could.

I climbed from my car and raced toward the door.

But before I reached it, someone stepped out onto the deck.

Two people, actually.

My heart pounded harder. Then I noticed it was Detective Sono . . . and Ezra.

Sono was okay.

Relief swept through me.

But it didn't last long.

Because if Ezra was here, then where was Danny?

"What are you doing out of your car?" Sono barked.

"I thought something had happened to you."

He gave me a look that would make the sun shrivel. "And you were going to help?"

"I can be very resourceful, I'll have you know." I glanced at Ezra. "Where is Danny?"

My renter only stared at me, almost as if in a trance.

A chill washed through me. Just what was going through that man's mind? Was he plotting ways to kill me? Feeling regret because he'd missed other opportunities?

"I'm going to take him down to the station," Sono said.

"I'll be right behind you."

He paused and gave me another fatherly stare. "That wasn't an invitation."

I shrugged, determined not to let this man get to me. "I know. But I don't need one. So I'll see you there."

chapter
thirty-five

"THIS EZRA GUY said he'll only talk to you," Sono muttered.

We were at the police station. I'd gone there, just as I'd said I would.

But I'd been denied entrance past the waiting room.

Instead, I'd camped out in the lobby, hoping someone would have mercy on me and give me an update.

Now, twenty minutes had passed before Sono reappeared and announced that Ezra only wanted to speak with me.

I was trying to look on the bright side, but I thought that maybe this could be a good thing.

"Only me?" I repeated, making sure I'd heard correctly.

Sono still looked annoyed as he stood near the doorway. "Are you comfortable being in there with him?"

"Am I going to be in there alone?"

"I'll be in there with you too."

I didn't hesitate before nodding. "Then yes."

A moment later, I was ushered into the room.

My throat tightened when I saw Ezra sitting there with a forlorn expression on his face.

The way his black hair was slicked back from his face sent another chill through me. Between his pale skin and blue eyes, I really thought there could be something to that vampire story I'd concocted.

But something about him right now looked different from his pictures. He was wearing nice jeans, a beige sweater, and a brown leather bomber jacket.

Strange . . . and somewhat familiar. But why? I couldn't put my finger on it.

Ezra spotted me, and hope filled his gaze.

But the look was only temporary.

"Joey . . . I just wanted a moment of your time." Ezra scowled at Sono. "Alone."

"That's not happening, buddy."

"Is that why you kept calling me over for various reasons?" I stood cautiously at the table, not wanting to give Ezra the satisfaction of seeing me sit.

Ezra scowled at Sono again.

Sono planted himself near the door, his arms crossed. "I'm not going anywhere. Get used to it. This is the best you've got."

"Why did you want a moment alone with me?" I asked Ezra.

"I wanted your advice. It's the whole reason I rented that house. I figured ten minutes alone with you would be worth how much it cost to rent it for a week."

Ten minutes alone with me? I shivered.

Then I remembered he'd said something about advice. "What did you want to talk to me about?"

"I'm trying to get my start in Hollywood. I've been cosplaying for a long time, and now I think I'm ready for the big time. I wanted to know if you had any tips for me."

"What?" Air rushed from my lungs. He had to be kidding me? But I knew he wasn't.

He nodded eagerly. "I've been a big fan of yours for a long time, and I want to make it big like you did. I was hoping you could give me some pointers. My dream is to be the next Sam Butler. I could even show you some scenes I've been practicing from *Relentless . . .*"

"That won't be necessary."

"No, really." His entire countenance changed into

that of an ultra-serious spy. "Raven, I thought I was going to lose you. Never do that to me again."

His imitation of Sam *was* pretty good.

Then it hit me—he was dressed like Sam right now.

"If that's true, why did you hide in your room when I stopped by to check on the water heater?"

His cheeks turned red. "I was going to surprise you with my imitation of Sam. I had everything set up, so I could reenact the final scene from the last episode of *Relentless*."

"The one where Sam proposes over dinner?"

He nodded a little too eagerly. "I had all the lines worked out. But then I got cold feet. Then you left. The next time you came, that guy was with you."

"And you were following me, weren't you?"

The red on his cheeks deepened. "I just kept losing my nerve."

"Why were you wearing a cape?"

"You remember that scene in season two, episode seven when Sam pretends to be Zorro and—"

"Saves the damsel in distress?"

Ezra's face brightened. "Yes, that's the one! I thought I could recreate it in the restaurant. But there were too many people. Too much could go wrong."

"Plus, wielding a sword in public isn't always smiled upon."

"You can say that again," Sono muttered.

I started to ask another question when Sono cleared his throat.

I needed to move this along more quickly, didn't I?

I stepped closer. "Ezra, what did you do with Danny?"

He snapped from his impromptu audition. "You mean that officer who came over?"

"Yes, that one."

He shrugged as if offended. "I didn't do anything with him. He barged into the house, which made be nervous. So I did what anyone in my shoes would do. I ran. I couldn't believe it when he chased me."

This guy was dense. "Then what happened?"

"I kept running until I hit some woods near the house."

"Nags Head Woods?" I suggested, thinking about the nature preserve not far away.

"Maybe. I wasn't exactly looking for any signs. It was all about self-preservation at that point. I just kept thinking: what would Sam do?"

He sounded crazy when he talked that way.

Then I realized I often asked myself what my alter-ego Raven Remington would do.

"I just kept running, and that cop kept following," Ezra continued.

"And then?" I encouraged.

"I eventually lost him. I hid in the woods until I thought it was safe to return to the house. It was pretty cold out there. But if Sam Butler could do it, so could I."

Note to self: talking about fictional characters as if they're real can make a person sound off-kilter.

Sono stepped forward, glowering at Ezra. "You don't know what happened to Officer Jones?"

"I have no idea. I only know he was chasing me. Those woods are bigger than I'd assumed, especially in the dark. It's easy to get turned around out there. A person could get lost out there for days."

I was familiar with those woods. I'd been out there before. It was more than a thousand acres, so I could see where someone might get lost.

Was that where Danny was now? Lost in those woods without shelter, proper clothing and food?

I prayed he was okay.

Sono promised to send teams back out to look for Danny.

I wanted to help, but he'd told me that under no uncertain terms was I allowed to do that. He said Jackson would have his head on a platter if he agreed.

I knew Jackson could be very convincing when it came to things like that, so I didn't argue.

Instead, I left the police station and ran to get a bite to eat. I hadn't had anything since breakfast.

Unfortunately, I was in the mood for comfort food. For that reason, I headed into my favorite local fried food establishment and grabbed a fish sandwich with tartar sauce, along with some hand-cut fries with plenty of salt and vinegar on them.

However, I wasn't about to scarf them down in public. No, thank you. No way would I give someone an opportunity to take a picture of me doing so and then post it all over social media.

Been there, done that.

I'd rather scarf down my food in the privacy of my car.

But as I stepped outside of the restaurant, I spotted someone leaning against my car in the dark.

I froze.

Maverick.

What was he doing here? Had he followed me?

"I'm not trying to scare you," he muttered as if reading my thoughts.

"Then why are you standing by my car? Was that you following me earlier?"

"What?"

Based on the totally perplexed look on his face, it

hadn't been him in the vehicle with the tinted windows. Besides, he seemed more the type to drive a huge pickup truck that he could go off-roading in.

"Never mind. What are you doing here?" After our earlier encounter, I'd had bad vibes about him. I wasn't sure exactly what his next move might be.

He straightened and turned toward me, his gaze pleading. "Don't do this movie."

"Why not?" I honestly wanted to hear his reasoning.

"Because Emma Jean was a good woman. She doesn't deserve to be portrayed the way that guy Bryant wrote about her in his book."

As soon as he said the words, realization spread through me. "You were Emma Jean's mystery man, weren't you?"

He ran a hand over his face. "When she moved back to the area the two of us got back together."

"Why is that a secret?"

He ran his hand over his face again. "It's complicated."

I would bet I could uncomplicate it. "You were dating someone else at the time, weren't you?"

"How'd you know?"

I shrugged. "Lucky guess."

"I didn't want people to know until Emma Jean and I knew for sure we could make our relationship work. I didn't want to have my heart broken again. Plus, there was the humiliation of being dumped. I'd never been dumped before Emma Jean. Frankly, I never want to be dumped again."

"So you were dating someone else, and you cheated on this woman with Emma Jean?" I clarified.

He nodded, but regret filled his eyes. "I was actually engaged. I know it was a slimy thing to do. And if I could go back . . ." He let out a long breath. "But it's too late for that now."

This wasn't a time for me to analyze his cheating ways. I had bigger fish to fry.

Speaking of fish . . . my sandwich was getting cold. But that was okay. I knew my priorities right now.

"What was Emma Jean like in the days before she died?" I watched Maverick as I waited for his answer.

"She seemed happy, to be honest. I think she liked life away from the limelight, despite how some people want to portray her."

"But she was about to be plunged back into the spotlight. She had a new record deal," I reminded him.

He shrugged. "She was trying to figure things out. But sometimes our biggest losses can actually be our biggest gains."

"So this whole suicide theory . . ."

He swung his head back and forth. "I don't believe

it for one minute. I never did. I mean, I know there was that note . . . but it just didn't feel right."

"So you think her death was an accident?"

"I'm not sure." His face tightened. "I've struggled with it ever since it happened. At first, I assumed it was. I mean, I didn't know of anyone who'd want to hurt Emma Jean. But as time has gone on, I've questioned it more."

"Did she have any enemies?"

"Other than her mother? Not really. But Emma Jean was acting weird the week before she died."

Maverick wasn't the first one to say that. Something must have happened to get her upset.

And to make her write that song.

I wasn't ready to give up the fact that I had that journal yet. But I would—as soon as I could figure out who to trust.

"Why were you so angry when you saw me in your office?" I asked.

"Because I think Emma Jean deserves better than that lousy movie. She was a good person. She just never had the chance to prove herself. Her life was cut short before she could." He shrugged. "I guess I wasn't sure whose side you'd be on. But my mom said you were nice and that I should talk with you."

I stared at Maverick. "One more thing: what did

your fiancée say about you and Emma Jean? Did she ever find out? Did you end up marrying her?"

He did the whole run-his-hand-over-his-face thing again. "No, I broke up with her after Emma Jean's death. I knew it wasn't fair of me to keep leading her on like that. But . . . I couldn't tell her the truth. I figured it was better if she didn't know I'd cheated. She might have suspected something, however. I'm not sure."

"Does this ex-fiancée still live around here?"

"She does. You've probably already met her."

I thought for a moment, and then my mouth dropped open. "Wait . . . you were engaged to Bobbi Sawyer, weren't you?"

He nodded. "Yes, Bobbi."

chapter
thirty-six

I HEADED BACK to my house, scarfing down my cold food on the drive.

The truth was that I didn't think Maverick had done it.

But what if Bobbi had found out that Maverick was cheating on her with Emma Jean?

People had killed for less reasons than that.

But I also remembered what medical examiner Raymond had said: most likely, it wasn't a woman who'd killed Emma Jean.

Bobbi could have been working with someone, however.

The thoughts continued to turn over in my mind.

I got to my house and climbed inside. I did my customary head rub with Ripley before letting him into the dog run. Then I fixed myself some hot choco-late and sat down on the couch.

My thoughts kept churning. So it appeared I could rule out Cyrus, Maggie, and now Maverick.

My pool of suspects was getting smaller and smaller.

But I still wanted to talk to Bobbi again. She'd never indicated she'd had a relationship with Maverick.

What else had she been hiding?

Her former best friend had been seeing her fiancée.

If Bobbi had found out, that would be a reason to be mad.

Plus, Bobbi would have been in the area when Emma Jean died.

I wasn't sure what I thought of that theory, but I wanted to let it keep playing in my mind.

Today had been full. Very full.

But I wasn't quite done yet.

I did a few quick searches until I found the number of Brent Mitchell.

On a whim, I called him. I knew he probably wouldn't answer, but I wanted to try anyway.

To my surprise, he did answer.

"Can I help you?" Music—loud music—played in the background, and I imagined him at rehearsal or in the middle of a recording session.

I explained who I was and what I was doing. I fully expected at any time that Brent might hang up on me.

But he didn't.

"You're asking about Emma Jean?" he repeated a little too loudly.

"I'm just trying to piece together her final days so I can perfect my imitation of her."

I found myself speaking equally as loud.

"We lost touch when she broke up with me and moved back home." More music blared, and Brent talked to someone in the background a moment before getting back to me. "It was probably for the best. We weren't really well suited for each other anyway."

"Is there anything you can remember about Emma Jean that might help me put together her mental state around the time she died?"

"All I know is that she was going to turn down that record deal she was offered."

"What? I thought that was what she wanted." At least that was the last thing I'd heard.

"We all did. But Emma Jean said she needed to figure out who she was away from the limelight and away from other people's expectations. She said she always felt as if she'd been pushed into singing and forced to be someone she wasn't. She wanted some time to explore who she was and who she wanted to be."

I could admire her for that. "So what was she going to do?"

"Last I heard, Emma Jean was going to focus on songwriting."

I let that settle. It was news to me.

And it was a very interesting development. Was that what Maverick was referring to when he said Emma Jean was still trying to figure out her future?

It just might be.

I'd talked to Jackson briefly before I went to bed that night, and he was doing fine. I couldn't wait to see him on Friday.

Before turning in for the night, I'd glanced out my front window. To my relief, I didn't see the man with a cigarette, which made me wonder if I'd just been seeing things that weren't there.

But I knew that wasn't the case.

I just didn't have an explanation for it.

And I didn't like not having answers.

Despite that, I'd managed to fall asleep.

When I awoke the next morning, I was full of a new determination.

Maybe today would be a good day, a day full of answers and no danger.

Even I knew the thought was ridiculous, however.

Danger seemed to be attracted to me, whether I went looking for it or not.

Before I could even roll out of bed, my phone rang. It was Jackson.

The fact that he was calling me in the morning sent up all kinds of red flags in my head.

"Is everything okay?" I rushed when I answered.

"Good morning, Joey. I didn't mean to upset you."

His calm voice slowed my heartbeat slightly. "I know you. I know if you're calling when you're not supposed to call then something happened."

"You're right." His voice remained reassuring. "But it's good news. Danny was found, and he's okay. It was like Ezra said, he was wandering in the woods."

My shoulders slumped as my muscles eased. "Thank goodness. What a relief."

"It is. I'm glad he's okay." Jackson paused. "But there's something else."

I waited, hardly able to breathe. "What?"

"Another attempt was made on Kitty last night."

"What?" Certainly, I hadn't heard him correctly. That was the last thing I'd expected.

"It's true. Someone dressed up as a doctor and snuck into her room. This man attempted to put something into her IV line, but a nurse walked in and stopped him. The man ran before the police could catch him. We now have an officer stationed outside her door."

"That's horrible." And brazen. I mean, someone really wanted that woman dead.

But why?

"It is. Someone wants her dead for a reason. Maybe because she knows something that she shouldn't. Maybe it's for another reason. Either way, I need you to be careful, Joey."

I pulled my blanket up toward my neck, suddenly chilled. "I will be. I promise."

So why did I feel like the odds were stacked against me?

chapter
thirty-seven

I KNEW EXACTLY what I wanted to do today.

I wanted to track down Bobbi.

I wasn't sure where to find her since I hadn't been successful the first time. But I was going to put more effort behind it this time.

I was also keenly aware of Emma Jean's journal. I'd taken pictures of the pages, and then I'd stashed the journal in a safe in my house.

I couldn't help but think there could be something valuable on those pages, and I didn't want the book to go missing—not that anyone else knew I'd found it.

Not to my knowledge, at least.

I really wanted to call one of my friends to see if they wanted to investigate with me. But I knew they were all working so it would just be me.

At most, I'd need to tread carefully.

But I remembered where I'd run into Bobbi last time—in downtown Manteo near some waterfront shoppes. I headed that way and wandered slowly down the brick sidewalk.

She gave music lessons. There was a good chance her studio was somewhere in this area.

I came to a strip of businesses located away from the retail area in a small alcove. One was an eye doctor. Another offered tutoring.

This would be the perfect place for a small music school.

I paused by a doorway and heard a lone guitar inside.

Could it be . . . ?

I glanced at the doorway, but there was no sign on it. However, a lone treble cleft sticker had been placed in the window.

Before I could talk myself out of it, I pushed the door open.

Two people sat in the middle of the room. Bobbi and a teenage girl who plucked out tunes on the guitar.

Bobbi's eyes narrowed when she saw me. "What are you doing here?"

"Can we talk?"

She scowled, and I wasn't sure what she would say.

"I figured it was only a matter of time until you figured things out," Bobbi said as she crossed her arms.

She'd dismissed her student, saying the lesson was over anyway.

As soon as the teenager was gone, I'd turned toward her. "You didn't tell me you were engaged to Maverick."

"You didn't ask."

I had so many retorts, but I didn't waste my breath with them.

Instead, I said, "I'm sure you were hurt when Maverick ended things."

"To say I was hurt would be an understatement." The first emotion cracked her face—sadness.

The woman was trying to be strong, but she was hiding her pain.

"Did you know about Emma Jean?" I asked softly.

She scowled. "I had my suspicions. I loved Maverick for a long time. Then Emma Jean started dating him in high school, even though she knew I had a crush on him. I decided to let it go back then. I was too insecure to step up and say anything. When Emma Jean left, I had his full attention. The two of us bonded over our loss, and I really thought we had a future together."

"How did you figure out he was cheating on you?"

"I knew something was up. He wasn't acting the same. I put it together that Emma Jean had moved back to town at the same time he started acting distant. Then one day I followed him." Bobbi let out a heavy sigh. "I saw him meet Emma Jean at her house. He gave her a big kiss, and that's when I knew they were back together."

"That couldn't have been easy to see."

Bobbi looked off in the distance and drew in a shaky breath. "Part of me wasn't surprised. It almost seemed planned, to be honest. Like they'd decided to get back together the moment she told him she was coming back."

"Were you angry enough to kill her?"

Bobbi blinked and shook her head. "No. Of course not. I'm more the type to get revenge by writing a mean song."

I studied her face. "Why do I feel like there's still something you're not telling me?"

She rolled her eyes and then let out a long sigh. I wasn't sure she was going to say anything.

Then she sighed again before blurting, "The morning before she died, I followed her. I was going to confront her. I wanted her to know that I wasn't stupid."

"What happened?"

"She went into this restaurant, and I was going to make a scene right then and there. Then she got a phone call and slipped out the back door. I followed her, curious about the call. Her whole demeanor changed when she saw the screen."

"And?" I was nearly holding my breath as I waited for her to finish.

"And as soon as I heard her tone, I knew something was wrong. She sounded upset."

"How so?"

"I could tell by her voice and her hushed tone. I heard her say she was going to meet someone that night." She paused. "Before I had a chance to make a scene like I wanted, some fans saw her and asked for her autograph. I decided to try another time. I never had the chance . . ."

"I guess not."

"I've suspected since then that the person she was meeting was the person who had something to do with her dying that night," Bobbi finished.

"What?" My voice pitched higher with emotion. "Why didn't you report that information?"

She rolled her eyes again, some of her softness disappearing. "I thought about it, but her death was ruled an accident. I figured I should let it go."

I stared at her another moment, wanting the truth

from her. "Are you sure you weren't the person meeting her?"

"Of course I'm sure." Her voice took on a new edge. "I didn't do anything like that to Emma Jean. Embarrass and humiliate her? Sure. But I couldn't have ever hurt her."

The real question was: did I believe her?

chapter
thirty-eight

AS SOON AS I finished speaking with Bobbi, Isaac texted. He wanted the cast and crew to meet back at the house used for filming in thirty minutes so he could give everyone an update.

I'd really hoped to have a free day today so I could keep investigating. I figured I could safely assume that no one on the cast or crew was responsible for Emma Jean's death. But I was more and more certain she'd been murdered.

Emma Jean had been fearful in the days up until she died, and someone had asked her to meet that night. I needed to tell the police that update. It could reopen this whole investigation.

I could see why Bobbi had wanted to keep that information quiet, especially given her track record.

But she would need to be questioned. Maybe she would even become a person of interest.

But Raymond thought a man was responsible for Emma Jean's death.

As far as Kitty's attack, that appeared to have been perpetrated by a man as well since it was a male who'd impersonated a doctor and snuck into her hospital room last night.

I had so many thoughts swirling inside my head right now, the last thing I wanted to concentrate on was this movie. But I knew this was what I'd signed up for and that I'd made a commitment. I had to follow through.

I did wonder if this meeting meant there was an update on Selby also. I figured we wouldn't continue filming as long as he was locked up or under suspicion.

Part of me was surprised that his arrest hadn't made national news yet. I figured it was simply a matter of time before a reporter got wind of it. That could potentially shut down this movie for good . . . or make it a blockbuster just because of the bad press alone.

Though I had a few minutes to spare, I decided to head to the house early. I didn't have time to do anything else.

When I pulled up, I noticed that no one else was here. Maybe that was a good thing. It would give me a moment to clear my thoughts and snap back into professional actress mode.

I parked then I headed toward the front door.

To my surprise, it was unlocked.

As I waited for everyone else to arrive, I sat on the couch and pulled up an old video of Emma Jean being interviewed. I began to watch as she talked about how being famous had changed her.

I paused the video a moment and went to my Kindle. I found the book Bryant had written on Emma Jean. So much of it had been the basis of this movie.

I skimmed through the pages. I'd already read the book once before filming.

Right now, I had to wonder if I'd missed any details. Details that could lead me to find the person who'd killed Emma Jean.

The book had come out about a year after Emma Jean's death, and it had been a bestseller. Bryant had done the media circuits to promote it. He'd been interviewed on talk shows and radio stations. If I remembered correctly, the unauthorized biography had remained number one on bestseller lists for at least a month.

This book really had launched the man's career.

I paused on one of the pages and read the words there.

Emma Jean thought of herself as being talentless—as

did others. Some even said she was the product of autotune on steroids. She grew up white trash and unloved. Even though she was a one-hit wonder, she was never meant for the big time. Unloved became the theme of her life.

Those were awful things to say about someone. Bryant should be ashamed of himself for publishing that.

My thoughts churned. This was all sensational . . . and the public had loved it. But the story was built on lies.

Lies that had benefited only one person.

A death that had benefited only one person.

My heart rate kicked up a notch.

The door at the front of the house opened, and I startled.

I hadn't even heard a car come down the driveway.

But when I looked up, I saw . . . Bryant James standing there.

My throat tightened until I felt as if I couldn't breathe.

The fact just the two of us were here wasn't a coincidence.

"If it isn't Joey Darling . . ." He closed the door and locked it behind him.

I forced myself to remain calm. "How did you get Isaac's phone and text me?"

"I don't know what you're talking about." A touch of satisfaction saturated his tone.

"I think you do." He wasn't going to play me anymore.

He shrugged, remaining near the door. "He may have left it on the table at the inn, and I grabbed it a moment."

A clearer picture formed in my head. "No one else is coming, are they? You wanted me here alone."

He leaned against the door.

My heart pounded harder when I realized what he was doing.

He was purposefully blocking my path to leave.

Why hadn't I told anyone else I was coming here?

But I knew. Because I thought I was heading to work. I didn't think I was walking into danger. At no time had I considered that maybe this was a trap.

That was clearly a mistake. A *huge* mistake.

How exactly would I get out of this one?

"Do you know why Emma Jean's book was so popular?" Bryant remained where he stood as he asked the question.

"Because she was a remarkable woman?"

"No, because she died. Stars who die young always

have a more intense level of fame than those who don't."

I couldn't argue with that statement. I'd thought the same thing earlier.

"I guess that was fortuitous for you. I can only assume you began the story before she died." As soon as the words left my lips, even more realizations filled me.

Bryant had started writing Emma Jean's book before she died . . . just like he'd started writing my book before I died.

He wanted to kill me, didn't he?

"I always like to have projects going on," Bryant crowed. "And I was fascinated with Emma Jean's story and her rise to fame, coming from nothing to reach the place where she was."

"Interesting . . . but that's still not telling me why you asked me to come here." I knew good and well why he'd asked me, but I needed to buy time.

Glancing around, I searched for a way out of the situation.

But I had none.

Jackson wasn't even here.

No, I was on my own now.

"All this sound equipment we have set up in this old house . . ." Bryant began fiddling with a lighting kit beside the door. "The wiring is so faulty, and the wood here is so brittle."

My heart pounded harder into my ears.

He planned on setting this place on fire to make it look like an electrical fire, didn't he?

"Why are you doing this?" I stared at him, desperation beginning to claw inside me. "All so you can finish writing that book on me and have another bestseller?"

"You don't think opportunities like that are just going to fall into my lap, do you? Sometimes you have to make your own fate."

"Or force someone else's . . ." I watched him continued to fiddle with the wiring. "Why here?"

"I thought it would be sadly poetic if you died on the filming location. *Tragically Relentless*, right? I thought it was clever. The whole premise will be that you were willing to do whatever it took to get ahead, even if it meant death itself."

"That's a little dramatic, don't you think?"

He shrugged. "Not really. I think it's going to be a blockbuster. Actor Joey Darling dies on set, canceling movie and ruining yet one more good thing."

I almost wanted to be offended by that, but I had too many other things on my mind.

"Why do you think people will assume that it's an accident?" I glanced around again, looking for anything I could use to defend myself with.

But there was really nothing. The only thing I had on me were my keys and phone.

The back door could serve as an escape route—if I could make a run for it. But by the time I got up and started that way, I knew Bryant could easily catch me.

I fought a frown—along with a good dose of despair.

What was I going to do?

chapter
thirty-nine

"I'M VERY good at making things look accidental."
Bryant sounded a little too smug as he said the words.
"Plus, everyone knows you have terrible luck and are
accident prone, so it just seems fitting."

This man wasn't just hungry for fame, success, and
money.

He was a cold-blooded killer. He'd lured Emma
Jean to her death.

Now he wanted to do the same to me.

I had to stop him.

I reminded myself to stay calm as I kept talking.
"You're good at making things look accidental? Just
like you made Emma Jean's death look accidental? She
went to the bridge that night to meet you, didn't she?"

Keep him talking. That always seemed like a good
plan.

Bryant raised his eyebrows. "You put that together, huh? You're smarter than I gave you credit for."

Jerk. I kept the thought silent.

As I sat there, my phone buzzed in my pocket. I desperately wanted to answer but couldn't. If only I'd told someone where I was going . . .

Thankfully, Bryant didn't seem to hear it.

For now, I kept talking. "If I had to guess, Emma Jean knew you were writing a book on her, and she didn't like some of the things you were going to say. For that reason, she offered to pay you off if you promised to stop writing that book."

He raised his eyebrows. "Very good, Mrs. Darling."

I resented his patronizing tone.

"You knew, however, that you'd make more money on this book if it hit the bestseller list than whatever amount she offered to pay you."

He smirked. "That's right. She said she had to watch her money now that she was leaving the music industry. I thought it was ridiculous. A copout. But we met, and one thing led to another. It all ended very tragically."

The way he said the words with so little emotion sent a chill through me. "I can only assume you wrote that suicide note and made sure it didn't get wet or blown away?"

My phone buzzed again. Who was calling me?

Maybe someone had realized I was missing and would look for me.

Maybe.

A grin spread across Bryant's face as he continued fiddling with the wires. "That's right. I typed it up before meeting her. I knew Emma Jean's voice pretty well by then, so I sounded exactly like her—if I do say so myself. I had a letter she'd sent to me once asking me to cease and desist from writing the book. I simply copied her signature. Something else I'm pretty good at doing."

"Well, aren't you clever?" This man was so cocky . . .

I reached into my jacket pocket and felt my phone. If only I could somehow figure out a way to call 911 without Bryant noticing.

But I knew that would be difficult.

However, I remembered how Emma Jean's song had begun playing on my phone when I had set my purse down—that night I thought she was haunting me. That was because my phone, even when I let it go to sleep, it still had a music player icon that popped onto the screen. It often did the same for podcasts and videos.

My thoughts raced as a plan formed in my mind.

Would it work?

I had no idea.

But it was worth a shot.

Because the last thing I wanted to be . . . was barbecued.

"How did you figure it out?" Bryant continued working as if this were just a normal day and we were having a normal conversation.

"I've been asking around," I admitted, my fingers fumbling over my phone screen. "That helped me."

"I should have given you more credit."

"But there is one other way I was able to figure things out."

"What was that?" He paused and glanced at me, appearing sincerely curious.

"It's the fact I've been able to channel Emma Jean."

He broke from his curious stare and scoffed at me. "What are you talking about?"

"I've been talking to Emma Jean a lot, and she's been talking back." The words sounded ridiculous coming from my lips, but I needed to be able to sell this. Acting 101 . . . it could save a life.

It had worked before, and I hoped it worked now also.

"You're crazier than I thought you were." Bryant shook his head.

He hadn't seen anything yet.

I really hoped I could sell this.

I fumbled sight unseen on my phone's home screen, trying to find what I hoped was a Play button there.

Sure enough, a second later Emma Jean's voice rang through my speakers.

I used all of my lip-syncing skills to pretend that her voice was coming out of my mouth.

"There are people in your life who will try to suck everything out of you," I mouthed along with Emma Jean. "People you can't trust. And it's a shame. With fame, it's hard to know who likes you for you and who likes you because they want something from you."

"What . . . ?" Bryant's face grew paler, and he let go of those wires as he stared at me as if unsure what was going on.

I rose, still moving my lips and not missing a beat. "But I've vowed to rise up against those people. My spirit will come back to haunt them one day. I promise you that."

He jerked.

As he did, sparks ignited from the light kit. In an instant, flames spread up the curtain.

I swallowed hard. I might be too late.

I couldn't waste any more time. I darted toward the back door.

But Bryant jumped into action and stayed on my heels.

He caught me by my shoulder and jerked me back.

The next thing I knew, my head collided with the wall.

Pain spread through my skull.

He wanted to knock me out.

Then he'd leave me here to die. People might even think this was another tragic accident.

Unless I did something to flip the script . . . but I would need to act quickly.

chapter
forty

AS MY HEAD SWAM, I fought drowsiness.

But I knew if I lost consciousness, this would be the end for me.

I couldn't let that happen.

Smoke already began to fill the air.

Bryant had been right.

This place was a deathtrap. Old, dry wood ripe for burning.

"You should have backed off," Bryant growled. "Then it might not be as painful for you."

Even with my eyes closed, I sensed a shadow above me.

Don't give in to the pain. Move!

My eyes popped open, and I saw Bryant holding a fire poker above his shoulder like a baseball bat.

Before he could slam it on my head, I rolled out of

the way.

He struck the wall instead.

He muttered under his breath and raised the poker again.

He was determined to finish this.

To finish *me*.

I quickly scrambled to my feet. I staggered forward but stopped, bending over to cough.

The smoke was already getting to me. The flames had begun to consume the walls and ceiling and quickly moved our way.

Bryant lunged at me again, an almost demonic look in his eyes.

But I ducked and scooted beneath him.

I reached the back door and desperately grasped the handle.

But it was locked.

No . . .

As I fumbled with the latch, Bryant grabbed me.

I knew exactly what he was going to do.

He wanted to ram my head into the wall again.

I fought against him. Tried to stop what was inevitably going to happen.

But he was too strong for me.

Then I remembered my signature move.

One that my dad taught me.

One we'd incorporated into *Relentless*.

I called it my baloney move.

Which really meant that, when in danger, I kicked my assailant below the knee.

Knowing I didn't have many other choices right now, I pulled my leg up. Then I rammed it as hard as I could into Bryant's leg.

His knee buckled, just as I'd hoped.

The move gave me enough time to scramble to the door.

This time, I unlocked it and threw it open.

Just in the nick of time.

The fire had reached the hallway.

It was just a matter of time before the whole place went up in flames.

I darted outside, only to collide with someone.

Fear filled me.

What now?

What if Bryant had brought backup?

"Joey? Are you okay?"

I looked up and blinked, unsure if there was smoke in my eyes causing me to see things. "Jackson?"

He lifted me into his arms. "Let's get you away from here."

"But I didn't think you . . ." As he swooped me up,

my head fell against his chest.

"I heard about what was happening here, and I sensed you needed my help. Looks like I got here in the nick of time."

"Bryant . . ." I pointed at the door. "He's still inside."

At just that moment, fire trucks and police cars pulled up to the property. Officials took control of the scene.

Several minutes later, two firefighters brought Bryant out, dragging him as they held him by his arms.

He was alive but in rough condition.

And I couldn't say he didn't deserve any of the pain he felt right now.

The movie set? I wasn't sure what they would do about that. But it wasn't my biggest concern at the moment.

Instead, I looked back up at Jackson. "How did you even know where I was?"

"It's that app you let me install on your phone. Find Friends. I texted you, but you must not have heard anything. That's when I decided to track you down myself."

I tightened my arms around him and nestled my head against his chest. "I'm so glad you did."

"Kitty woke up and identified Bryant as the person who shot her. She saw him when she came on set this week and recognized him from five years ago. She'd seen him in town in the days before Emma Jean died, and she put the pieces together."

That was good news, at least.

"Plus, there's a witness who overheard Emma Jean saying she was going to meet someone at the bridge that night," I added. "That person was Bryant. He admitted to me that he wrote Emma Jean's suicide note and that he went to meet her with the intention of ending her life. All so his book could be a bestseller."

Jackson shook his head. "That's one of the most twisted things I've ever heard."

I had to agree.

Paramedics surrounded me on either side.

"They need to check out that knot on your head," Jackson said.

I knew better than to argue. Plus, I did have a pounding headache.

I reluctantly removed my arms from around Jackson.

But I was so glad he'd shown up . . . just in the nick of time.

Could I have stumbled and fumbled my way to safety on my own?

Probably.

But I needed someone to catch me when I fell.

And I always knew Jackson was up for the task.

chapter
forty-one

THAT NIGHT, I'd never been so happy to be tucked on my couch with Jackson on one side of me and Ripley on the other.

After the paramedics had cleared me, the police had taken my statement.

Selby had been released. He'd already sent a text about it to the cast and crew. He'd told everyone he'd been rightfully cleared and that we'd need to pivot concerning production.

He wanted to meet with everyone tomorrow.

He'd sent me a personal text to say thank you.

So had Isaac.

After hearing about the fiasco at the rental house —and my vampire theory—Jackson had run over to check on it. He'd also had a stern talk with Ezra.

Jackson had found the cross I'd assumed Ezra had

taken down because of his undead status. Turned out the nail had come out of the wall, and the cross had fallen behind a table.

The trash bags? They'd been legitimately used for trash. And the rope was for a game of tug of war Ezra was planning with some cosplay friends later.

The dinner had been set up for me—but only because Ezra was hoping to get some acting advice.

I was so glad Jackson was back and could handle these things now.

"You feeling okay?" Jackson studied my face with that tender look in his eyes.

I nodded, which only made my headache slightly worse. "I'm fine. I'm glad you're here. Really glad."

"Me too. I heard about the man you saw outside the house. Any updates you haven't told me about?"

I remembered him too and shook my head. I'd found answers to a lot of my questions, but not that one. "No. Maybe it was nothing."

"Could it have been Adolf?"

I'd thought about that. "Maybe. It seems like something he might do. I don't plan on finding him to ask."

"Did you open the letter yet?"

I remembered what Bryant had written in the book about who my real father was. I had to believe he'd just made that all up. "Not yet."

"You will when you're ready."

My lungs loosened. I was so glad Jackson understood. Those DNA results were something I needed to explore on my own time.

Then I remembered Emma Jean's journal that I'd found.

"One minute. I need to show you something." I popped up and ran to retrieve it.

Then I sat on the couch and explained to Jackson how I'd found it.

I flipped to that last song and showed Jackson the lyrics. "Bryant must have been threatening Emma Jean in the week before she died. That's why she had agreed to meet with him, never anticipating what would happen. But the lyrics here show how frightened she was. Bryant scared her. Really, all she wanted to do was disappear from the limelight for a while, but this book would have changed that."

"Good work, Joey," Jackson muttered, pushing a hair behind my ear. "But I'm really second-guessing if I ever should leave you alone again."

I grinned. "It's probably a good idea if you don't."

As I started to close the journal, I noticed a small pocket attached to the inside of the back cover. A paper had been tucked into it.

Out of curiosity, I opened it.

The handwriting matched Emma Jean's.

I read aloud, "In the unlikely event of my death, I'd like my house to go to Glenn Pumpernickel. He supported me and my music when I was younger and never expected a single thing in return. I've never forgotten his kindness. I know his wife has cancer and that they're facing financial hardships. I've been keeping my eye on the situation and trying to find out ways to help. I hope I live to be old, into my eighties. But if I don't, I want my house to go to the one person who liked me for me."

Tears filled my eyes as I read the words.

"That's beautiful," I murmured.

"I don't know who this Glenn guy is, but he sounds incredibly selfless."

"I guess I need to turn this evidence in to the police," I murmured.

"Yes, but I'll see if you can be the one to tell Glenn the good news. I'm sure there will be some lawyers involved to make sure this is all legit. But it sounds like maybe Emma Jean's house can finally come out of probate."

"Kitty won't be happy."

"I think Kitty is doing just fine for herself." He shifted, his gaze turning more serious—and more personal. "Joey, why didn't you just call me if you needed help? Why try to handle everything alone?"

Cement suddenly filled my lungs. "I don't know . .

. I guess I just wanted to prove to you that I could handle things. That I'm not a . . . pampered princess."

He cocked his head to the side. "You're letting that article get to you?"

I shrugged. "Maybe. I mean, I don't want to seem incompetent."

"You don't."

I glanced up at him. "You mean that?"

"I do."

"But I'm always messing up and getting myself into sticky situations."

He leaned closer and kissed my forehead. "And that's just one more thing to love about you. But I'm always here if you need me. *Always*. Promise me you'll always let me know if you need me."

I tucked myself next to him and nodded. "I will. I promise. No more blunders."

"I love you, Joey Darling Sullivan."

"And I love you too."

also by christy barritt:

you might also enjoy

...

The Squeaky Clean Mystery Series

On her way to completing a degree in forensic science, Gabby St. Claire drops out of school and starts her own crime-scene cleaning business. When a routine cleaning job uncovers a murder weapon the police overlooked, she realizes that the wrong person is in jail. She also realizes that crime scene cleaning might be the perfect career for utilizing her investigative skills.

#1 Hazardous Duty
#2 Suspicious Minds
#2.5 It Came Upon a Midnight Crime (novella)
#3 Organized Grime
#4 Dirty Deeds
#5 The Scum of All Fears
#6 To Love, Honor and Perish
#7 Mucky Streak

I'm not really a private detective. I just play one on TV.

Joey Darling, better known to the world as Raven Remington, detective extraordinaire, is trying to separate herself from her invincible alter ego. She played the spunky character for five years on the hit TV show *Relentless*, which catapulted her to fame and into the role of Hollywood's sweetheart. When her marriage falls apart, her finances dwindle to nothing, and her father disappears, Joey finds herself on the Outer Banks of North Carolina, trying to piece together her life away from the limelight. But as people continually mistake her for the character she played on TV, she's tasked with solving real life crimes . . . even though she's terrible at it.

about the author

USA Today has called Christy Barritt's books "scary, funny, passionate, and quirky."

Christy writes both mystery and romantic suspense novels that are clean with underlying messages of faith. Her books have sold more than four million copies and have won the Daphne du Maurier Award for Excellence in Suspense and Mystery, have been twice nominated for the Romantic Times Reviewers' Choice Award, and have finaled for both a Carol Award and Foreword Magazine's Book of the Year.

She is married to her Prince Charming, a man who thinks she's hilarious—but only when she's not trying to be. Christy is a self-proclaimed klutz, an avid music lover who's known for spontaneously bursting into song, and a road trip aficionado.

When she's not working or spending time with her family, she enjoys singing, playing the guitar, and exploring small, unsuspecting towns where people have no idea how accident-prone she is.

Find Christy online at:
www.christybarritt.com
www.facebook.com/christybarritt
www.twitter.com/cbarritt

Sign up for Christy's newsletter to get information on all of her latest releases here: **www.christybarritt. com/newsletter-sign-up/**

facebook.com/AuthorChristyBarritt
x.com/christybarritt
instagram.com/cebarritt